THE BOTTLE

A wine story

THE BOTTLE - *A wine story*

This is a work of fiction. Almost all names and characters given and all the episodes narrated are figments of the author's imagination and are not to be considered real.

Even the rare instances of characters with real people's names - towards whom the writer feels infinite esteem - are to be considered fictitious characters, the traits and occurrences narrated of which are also a figment of the author's imagination for the delight of the readers.

Therefore, any resemblance of the story to facts, scenarios, organizations, or people, living or deceased, real or imaginary, is completely coincidental.

To those who do not drink the last bottle of wine simply because they wouldn't have any left

To those who love natural wines and those who believe natural wine does not exist.

To those who claim all great wines are French and those who find great wines everywhere.

To all people who love wine and the fine pleasures of life.

CHAPTER 1

*"Great is the fortune of he who possesses a good bottle,
a good book, and a good friend."*
Molière

Observing what was now a ritual, Tommaso stopped a step away from the *Wine Room* door, closed his eyes, and held his breath for a couple of seconds. He then exhaled, along with all the thoughts and worries of that day. Just before those worries could return, he entered the *Wine Room* and took the long staircase that led to the underground chamber, plunging into the reassuring dimness produced by soft lighting and stone arches. As he walked down the steps, he couldn't help but hear the pleasant piano music in the background, which was perfectly in tune with the warm atmosphere of the place.

The *Wine Room* was a panacea for the soul. The tiny dark wooden tables, the exposed chestnut beams, the smell of gourmet food, and the sought-after collection of wines spread out on the shelves along the wall exuded a kind of consoling beauty. He gazed at the bottles from all over the world, carefully divided by region. Italy and France were his favorites, followed by the New World wines, with the United States leading the way. Scattered around the small rooms, amid clay amphorae and straw fiascos arranged on old solid wooden shelves, hung oil paintings depicting vineyards with stone towers and small hilltop farmhouses.

His attention was drawn to the small collection of wine-making manuals available to customers. These manuals were constantly updated by the owner of the restaurant during his trips abroad.

Upon entering the main room, he spotted someone seated at a table wearing a familiar blue shirt. In turn, that person recognized him and waved at him.

"Good evening!"

"Hi Luciano, sorry I'm late. Have you been waiting long?"

"Just a few minutes. I took the liberty of ordering two glasses of Franciacorta wine."

As Tommaso took a seat, his friend handed him a half-full goblet of wine.

"Excellent choice. Sorry, I got held up...."

"Oh! Come on, stop right there! Fun first, then duty."

Tommaso willingly obeyed. He took off his glasses, loosened the knot of his tie, and sipped the Franciacorta. He found it refreshing and zesty. He closed his eyes to savor it properly. He pictured the grapes ripening under the sun and being washed by the rains.

Almost fifty, handsome and unfailingly impeccable in his role as sales manager at an international insurance company, Luciano stared at him, smiling. He ran a hand through his straight hair before snapping back to reality.

"While I wait for you to give me your opinion on the wine, I must tell you that I had lunch with Caterina today."

"How is she?" asked Tommaso instinctively, still immersed in his visions.

"I think well. In fact, great! She's seeing a new guy."

Tommaso opened his eyes again and raised an eyebrow.

"Really? And she told you this casually?"

Luciano shrugged his shoulders.

"Well, not really. Monica told me before. However, when I mentioned it, Caterina limited her response to an 'mh-mh,' which I took as a yes."

Tommaso took another sip of his wine.

Blessed are the grapes! he thought. It is easier for them.

"Anyway, I suggested to her that we should take him out to a nice dinner one day, and deep down, she seemed pleased," Luciano continued. "Of course, she was vague. Go figure. However, when I drove her back home and invited her to introduce him to me sooner or later, she smiled."

Tommaso proposed a toast with a wine glass half full. "To Caterina and her new boyfriend!"

"To teenage daughters, to trouble and love, which is the biggest trouble of all."

After updating him on the latest news, Luciano focused on the wine.

"So, you're not going to tell me anything about what we're drinking?"

One of the typical pastimes of wine lovers is trying to guess the wines blind. The two friends were no different, despite their terrible results.

Dew on the stems pondered Tommaso. *Warm rays stretching without haste, caressing the skin of each individual grape.*

"Fresh, tangy, and it has an impressive wine length. I don't see any colors or reflections that suggest a pinot noir, so I'd say blanc de blancs. It's a chardonnay."

"Exactly! It's the brut of Casa Caterina. They've just put it on the menu. What about you, though? How are things going at the law firm?"

Tommaso placed the wine glass on the table and regretfully left the sunny vineyards that Franciacorta vividly summoned in his mind.

"There's progress. Things are going well. We have an important case."

"Is that guy still being an asshole?"

Tommaso shrugged.

"He's not being an asshole. That's his job."

"Screwing over clients? Really?"

"Bringing home the contracts," he replied.

Luciano nodded to the waiter, who responded with a look of agreement.

"Trust me. I've seen many like him. They are the worst. They play safe, so you trust them and let them do it. And within a few months...bam, their name is on the door, and you have to find another firm."

"I don't think that's the case," Tommaso tried to downplay it without much conviction. "And, anyway, the music is about to change."

Marcello interrupted them, asking them what wine they were planning to continue with.

Piedmont, Langhe. Gaja Rossj Bass 2003. The evening was just beginning to get interesting.

"Let's also have a portion of crostini with butter and anchovies and two cuts of tuna steaks with pepper and wasabi," Luciano added, getting back to the task at hand as soon as the orders had left for the kitchen. "So, this new case?"

"Harassment at work," Tommaso quickly replied, happy that the focus of the discussion was no longer his relationship with his associate.

"Of course, your friend has such questionable taste!" retorted Luciano, showing that he had no intention of giving up the fight.

"I mean one customer. Actually, three."

"A class action? Interesting."

"The molester is the general manager of a general hospital."

Luciano burst out laughing.

"You get the big doctor! And you're going to take him to court?"

"I've already had a chat with the hospital lawyers. They offered two hundred thousand euros each as compensation for settlement."

"Does the young lawyer Mariani get an award and run away with it?"

The new wine arrived just in time for the toast. The waiter presented it to them. After receiving a gesture of approval, he pulled out the corkscrew, cut off the capsule, uncorked the bottle, and handed Tommaso the glass for tasting.

As he brought the glass up to his nose, the boy recalled reading an interview with a winemaker.

In the article, the winemaker stated that to appreciate the wine, one must pour it into a large container to let it oxygenate before refilling the bottle and letting it rest for a few more hours. Not having that much time on his hands, he simply inhaled carefully before taking a small sip.

"Excellent, thank you," he said contentedly.

The wine, which was deep gold in color and had a light but fragrant floral bouquet mixed with an intense aroma of pastry cream, had immediately enchanted him with its perfect mix of elegance and power. Marcello moved on to fill Luciano's goblet, who, after taking a sip, extolled its qualities and great depth of flavor. Then he topped up Tommaso's glass and placed the bottle in an ice bucket.

"What were we saying? Ah, yes, of course. The bulk of the prize for young Mariani will be reinvested in the studio as agreed because, in the first year, we will have to clench our teeth. What is important, however, is that I close the case with that client. In short, it will appear in the records that that money is coming in thanks to me."

"That's my shark! It's all a power play. I see you've figured it out. As in marriage."

"Did you ever say that to Monica? No wonder she dumped you."

"Consensual separation," Luciano clarified, pointing his index finger at him.

"Right. And I'm an equal partner."

The waiter returned to the table again to ascertain whether the wine was to their liking.

"In a few weeks, however, we will be meeting with the owner of a company that makes engines for all kinds of boats," Tommaso continued when they were alone again.

"That will be a crucial meeting. If he becomes our client, the firm would be consolidated, and we could stop navigating by sight to keep on topic." He paused briefly, then exclaimed, "I have an idea."

"Shoot!"

Tommaso remained silent for a few seconds, wondering if his friend would consider him naive. Even though he had his own troubles, with a divorce on his shoulders and a daughter who barely spoke to him, Luciano was a real hustler at work. He was always driving home important results with a cheery smile and the typical savoir-faire of someone who is naturally inclined to sales and was highly appreciated by his superiors. He had managed, by way of production bonuses, to cover a good part of the separation expenses. His devotion to his work played a considerable role in this. So, how would he judge his stunt from the height of that experience?

"I thought of organizing a tasting in the office," suggested Tommaso.

Luciano watched him in silence.

"With fine wines," his friend hastened to add. "And paired tastings, a sommelier to serve...in short, a real professional tasting. Except it will be held inside the office."

After another very long pause, Luciano gave his blessings to the idea.

"Beautiful!"

"Really? Doesn't that seem a bit over the top?"

"No. The client needs to feel pampered, and overdoing it is fine. A firm that goes to the trouble of organizing a luxury tasting in your honor conveys two pieces of information; it has resources to invest and attention to devote to you. Two very good business cards."

"That's what I was hoping for."

"Now, let's think about the wines."

"What wines?"

"The wines to offer. You certainly won't be able to serve just any wines! Last month I went to a tasting in Düsseldorf and tasted a 2005 Château Lafite-Rothschild. It was quite memorable! I think it costs more than a thousand euros. Alternatively, for less than half of that, you can buy a 2004 Vega Sicilia Único. A client sent me a few bottles."

"How do you get clients to give you such expensive wines?"

"I pamper and compliment them. To this guy, in particular, I confessed that one of my biggest regrets is that I didn't buy a BMW Z4 like his when I had the chance, and for that, I envied him a lot. Two weeks later, I received the bottles along with a brochure from his trusted BMW dealer."

"And the Vega Sicilia is less than five hundred euros, you say?" asked Tommaso, starting to do the calculation mentally.

"Exactly, too little. You're in danger of coming across as cheap."

"That's right, I was just about to tell you that," replied Tommaso wryly.

"You always have to think on the bright side. You could enjoy a Clos du Mesnil and put one thousand five hundred euros in the studio account."

"Don't exaggerate! Anyway, I'll have to talk to Piergiorgio about it too."

"Yes, talk to Piergiorgio about it. I bet he'll swipe your idea and sell it as his own."

Tommaso laughed a little forcibly.

"You're right. We should buy the Clos du Mesnil ourselves and chug it."

Luciano shrugged.

"I would never spend that kind of money on wine."

"But you just suggested I do the opposite."

"For business, sure. But on a personal whim, it seems too much. I believe a thousand or two thousand euros can be better invested."

"You mean you wouldn't like to go on a spree at least once in your life?"

"Two thousand euros is not insane… I would rather call it a cheap insanity. It's neither fish nor fowl."

"Right, let's raise the bar," Tommaso prompted him, pulling out his smartphone and quickly typing into Google. "Ornellaia, jéroboam, 2013: one thousand one hundred euros."

"Absolutely not! I've never liked large formats."

"Brunello di Montalcino Biondi Santi, 1957 Reserve, six hundred."

"We can do better than that. Check this out!"

Luciano turned and showed Tommaso his phone.

"Naturally, I would never do that, but if I had to splurge once in my life, I would aim for something like that. If you're going to do damage, it might as well be memorable."

Tommaso barely heard his friend's words. His eyes were glued to the white label in the foreground at the auction portal open on Luciano's smartphone and to the dark wine glimpsed in the transparency of the glass. Romanée-Conti, 1991. Bumped for twenty-five thousand euros.

Twenty-five thousand euros!

How memorable could the mere existence of a grape intended for such a wonder be? What ecstasy could the palate of the lucky man who had tapped into such a source of bliss have known?

"…pan and visit the country far and wide."

Tommaso snapped back from his daydream.

"What?"

"I said, if I had twenty-five thousand euros to spend, I would take the family to Japan and visit the country far and wide."

"The family?"

"You know what I mean. Come on. Caterina and Vicky."

Victoria, Luciano's new girlfriend, lived in Milan and worked in a publishing house. She was a few years younger than him, but she was very straightforward and opinionated. After just four months of dating, she had suggested that he move to Milan with her because she hated Rome for its slow-paced, countryside vibes, and Luciano went into a meltdown.

"In fact, you know what?" he added, scratching his chin thoughtfully. "I really should arrange something like that. I've been neglecting Cate, and I'd like her and Vicky to get to know each other better. Then maybe she will learn to love this city because I'm not going to Milan, no way in hell! I have a daughter here, and even though my relationship with her mother is over, the one I have with Caterina will never end. Maybe it's too early to go to Japan, but a little trip to some European capital this summer, when Cate is on her study break, would work..."

"Isn't she attending university now?" interrupted Tommaso.

"Yes!" Luciano replied, full of pride. "First year, Modern Literature."

"So, she will have exams in the summer."

"Not in August. At least that's what she told me."

"It will be her only month off from the academic year. I bet she can't wait to drop everything and go away with you and Victoria. I think Cate might have other plans, you know? She's 20 years old, Luciano. Remember when you were 20?"

"Whose side are you on? Of course, I remember my twenties, but being younger, you should remember them better than I do. Anyway, you never say no to a free vacation."

"What if we bought ourselves a bottle of Romanée-Conti to celebrate the fact that there is nothing to celebrate?"

Tommaso looked around to see where this sudden proposal had come from just before he realized that he had made the suggestion on the spur of the moment.

"Are you crazy?"

Luciano looked at him blankly.

He could have been. Perhaps, though, not too much, either.

"I know it sounds absurd," Tommaso said. "And it probably is. But don't you ever feel like doing something crazy, something you'll remember forever? Just like you would have done in your 20s if only you had the job you have today and the knowledge that..."

Tommaso had not prepared that speech. He just went with the flow. Yet the words came out on their own, and each sounded more convincing in his head than the last. Luciano placed his hands on the table and put his fingertips together.

"Do you happen to have twelve thousand five hundred euros to spend, Attorney Mariani? Not because it is an impossible amount, but..."

"No, I don't have them, but we don't necessarily know if all bottles of Romanée-Conti would cost that much. Maybe we can find one at a more affordable price. We could do some research and see if we get lucky."

"Lucky? Did you just seriously utter the word lucky in front of me?"

Luciano laughed so loud that the customers sitting at the nearby table turned to look at him.

"Everything I've had in life, I've earned by working day and night. Luck is overrated, my friend. Let it go."

Tommaso ignored his friend's protests and logged on to Wine Auction Ltd, one of the best wine auction sites.

Sometimes, in the evening, he'd usually log in there and browse through the lots of the various auction houses that the portal brought together. He tidied up the search field and watched the loading bar color itself with the exhausting slowness of internet connections in underground places. When the page finally loaded, he interpreted what appeared as a divine sign.

"Romanée-Conti 1991," he announced. "The auction ended, and there's an unsold bottle at Tate Ward Auctions House in London. We're buying it directly online, so we can save on travel costs. I would say this option is particularly attractive, considering the final price, twelve thousand euros."

Luciano continued sipping his chardonnay, carefully thinking about what Tommaso had said.

"You agree that this is a sensational opportunity! I'm checking past lots. The auction bases were all around twelve to fifteen thousand. This is a sign of destiny. That makes it six thousand each."

"A very good opportunity," agreed Luciano. "But it's still six thousand euros more than I intend to spend on a wine."

Not even Tommaso could afford that expense lightly. At least not at that moment. Unless.

"Julie!" he exclaimed.

"Are you serious?"

"Julie is a real wine enthusiast," continued Tommaso without batting an eye, who now clearly saw the pieces of the mosaic of fate being composed before his eyes, revealing an increasingly defined pattern.

"She works in a wine store. We could ask her to buy the wine with us."

"We?"

"In that way, we come down to four thousand each. It's doable. It's not easy, but we can come up with something."

Luciano emptied his glass and stretched.

"Of course, nothing could be easier when laughing and joking. My dear chap, it's half past ten, and I still have some work to do, so I must say goodbye. Sleep on it, and you'll see that you'll get over it by tomorrow. See you at the tasting on Saturday, okay? Let me know how it goes tomorrow with the harassment case."

"All right. Leave it. It's on me."

"There you go, that's the spirit!"

Chapter 2

"Life is too short to drink bad wine."
Johann Wolfgang von Goethe

It turned out to be a gloomy Monday for Tommaso in the Prati neighborhood, where the Pizzi & Mariani studio was located. It was on the second floor of a period building.

Tommaso's rented studio, which cost an arm and a leg, was also on the same floor. On the same landing stood the entrances for a public notary and the building manager's apartment, someone Tommaso had never seen. Once again, he felt like a stranger in that large, cold city. It wasn't so much because of the climate but because of the distance from one another. People were committed daily to avoiding plummeting into an asphalt pothole while running to get to work on time. The two active subway lines and a chaotic and disorganized transport system just made matters worse.

With a general sense of discomfort, he slipped the key into the keyhole and entered the studio.

The decor was still quite spartan, devoid of those few but essential elements of elegance required to make it a cozy place. Things such as plants, landscape paintings, and a few colorful objects could radiate some warmth. Not to mention a few good bottles to sip on occasion with top clients or to celebrate winning important cases. As soon as he was inside, he noticed Piergiorgio's gray coat hanging in the doorway.

Unbelievable! It was nine o'clock, an hour and a half before the first appointment of the day, and his senior colleague was already there. The plan to arrive at the office early enough to go over one's part in solitude and get into the right mindset had been nipped in the bud.

Talk about being workaholics. Maybe I should learn from him, he said to himself. Preparing for a case with Pizzi around was out of the question. He would look like a rookie. Before he could sneak off to one of the many bars in the neighborhood where he could check his papers undisturbed, Piergiorgio popped up at the end of the hallway, greeting him with a beaming expression.

"Good morning, Tommaso. You're early too? Nice to see you!"

A mere five years older than him, Pizzi had spent that time working in a prominent law firm, within which he had made a name for himself as well as a solid scaffolding of cynicism. It was precisely as a result of that experience that he had agreed to open the firm with Tommaso, provided that he held the reins in the first year. Although they were lawfully equal partners, it had been made clear from the beginning who among the two could afford to drop everything and walk away with their clients.

"Good morning, Piergiorgio. Did you sleep well?"

"Very well, thank you. Shall I make you some coffee?"

The question surprised Tommaso. It was the first time since they had opened the firm over seven months earlier that his partner had offered to make him coffee, thus reversing roles. He wondered whether Piergiorgio's sudden kindness was because he had shown up so early at the office or because of his skill in handling the case of the three women who had been harassed at work, who were to arrive that morning to sign the contract. Beyond the particular reason, he felt that the oddness of the moment was worth an overdose of caffeine.

"Yes, Thank you. With a dash of milk."

"Coming right up. If the morning is any indication, this is going to be a very good day."

"Oh yeah?" Tommaso took off his jacket and hung it next to his gray coat, hell-bent on letting his partner's good spirits rub off on him. "What happened that was so interesting?"

Pizzi inserted the coffee pod into the machine, placed the cup under the dispenser, and lowered the lever. A powerful aroma of arabica permeated the room.

"We closed the deal. The Polyclinic."

Before he could assimilate the information, Tommaso was just in time to extend his hand toward the steaming cup his colleague was handing him. However, his hand froze midair, as did his smile.

"I beg your pardon?"

"The chief, Mr. nimble hand. The three employees at the hospital. The three *clients*, it might be better to call them now."

"But...the appointment was at 10:30."

"Sorry, you're right. I forgot to notify you. They called last night to ask to bring it forward to eight o'clock when you were already off. You told me you were going for drinks with a friend, so I thought it wasn't worth bothering you."

Now Piergiorgio's smile bore a tinge between accomplice and fatherly and appeared to say, "You don't have to thank me, don't worry. I'm the experienced partner here. It's only natural that I take on the responsibility of bringing home the bacon while you're out getting drunk."

Tommaso continued to smile in turn, although his face became more like one of those scary guffawing Halloween masks. When he realized that he had not yet taken the coffee from his colleague's hands, he regained control of his hand and grabbed the cup, finding himself defeated at that very moment.

"But why didn't you send me a message?"

"It was a total waste to have you come here two hours earlier just to gather a few signatures. I took care of that. Ah, by the way, Elisa, the one with black hair and a big nose, says hello. I think she likes you," he concluded with a wink.

"Well, I..."

"Come on, don't look like that! It's all work that goes in for the firm, and that's what's important. Whether the signature is mine or yours makes no difference. Now come on, while we're here, let's get down to business. To work!"

Tommaso nodded weakly.

"You're right. Ah..."

"Tell me?"

Tommaso hesitated for a moment before talking again.

"There's no milk in the coffee."

Pizzi looked at the cup and nodded seriously.

"True. We're out of milk."

CHAPTER 3

"Some never go crazy. Their wines must be boring."
Charles Bukowski

Tommaso walked out of the subway and crossed Piazza dei Cinquecento, taking his sweet time and enjoying the pleasant mid-October weather. Rome glowed under the autumnal sun. The bluish sky was only speckled with the flights of doves, making swirls around the golden Virgin Mary of a church, then descending to the statue of Pope John Paul II and finally gliding across the square between taxicabs, buses, and the legs of hundreds of people intent on getting in and out of the station. Moving forward along the polished pavement, he observed the cars jammed at the traffic lights in front of Via Cavour and the eclectic chaos that brought the square to life, with taxi drivers standing outside their cars waiting for customers and the smell of freshly baked bread. A group of German tourists in shorts, colorful tank tops, flip-flops, and shopping bags walked past him, laughing and waving brochures advertising fixed-menu restaurants on Via Nazionale.

It was almost lunchtime, and there was a smell of food in the air. Tommaso caught himself smiling for no apparent reason. Even though everything in his life was not going perfectly, that morning was too bright and promising to be sad. He hurried across the street and stopped at the book and record stands in front of the Baths of Diocletian, regretting having worn his jacket. The long Roman summer that sprawled into early autumn did not go well with the formal attire and rigor of certain professions.

To be honest, I could really use a few days of leisure, he thought as he carefully sifted through old copies with ruined covers of "Urania," "Segretissimo," and "Tex" in pastel colors.

At the bottom of the pile, he uncovered a dusty white tome with a red goblet in the background and a title that made his eyes sparkle: *The Encyclopedia of Wine, 2001 edition.*

He blew the dust off the cover and turned the book over. The back cover read, "a useful tool for learning about the subject of 'wine' from every possible perspective, from winemaking to wine classification, from historical and cultural profiles to tasting."

Even though these were topics he had heard and seen before, he purchased the book for his collection anyway.

"How much is it?" he asked the wispy head hidden behind a stack of books.

"It is written inside," replied the old man without even looking up.

Tommaso paid and made his way back, intending to flip through his new purchase immediately with a glass of wine and Julie.

At lunchtime, the enoteca, aka wine bar, on Via Cavour was packed as usual, but not for him. Undeterred by the stares of customers waiting to be seated, he made his way through the tables and joined the young woman polishing a set of crystal stemware/crystal grand ballon glasses behind the counter. Amid the hustle and bustle, he picked up a Zero 7 song called "Swing" in the background that he particularly liked.

"There you are! I reserved you the usual little spot by the window. How are you, Tom?"

Julie looked radiant as always. She was wearing a white cotton blouse with the sleeves rolled up to the elbow, black pants, and the ever-present burgundy-colored apron with the logo of the wine bar. Her long hair pulled back into a high ponytail, framed her glowing face adorned with light makeup.

"Thank you, you're a sweetheart. I'm fine, I could be better, but I don't want to complain."

"The usual charcuterie board, then?"

"Yes."

"And...?"

" Today, I'm up for a Chardonnay."

"And what kind of Chardonnay would that be?"

"Elegant and well suited for aging."

Julie laughed, drawing attention from a group of young men seated a short distance away.

"I'm not kidding," Tommaso continued. Intimidated, he scratched his nose. "That's how I feel today."

"Chardonnay it is. Have a seat, and I'll bring you everything in a bit."

The small table reserved for him was in the far corner of the bar, near the large window that looked out onto the street. A tiny vase with blue paper flowers was in the center, and the menus were stacked neatly off to the side.

Tommaso's smartphone screen lit up with Luciano's confirmation of their meeting on Saturday. Tommaso immediately replied to his friend.

"I'm at Julie's! I just picked up another book."

"Did you tell her about the bottle?"

"Not yet. I just got here and haven't been able to talk to her yet."

"Okay, call me then!"

At that moment, the girl arrived with the wine, a ruby-colored felt coaster, a tin box with napkins, and a round charcuterie board filled with delicacies. She gently placed on the table a Renano glass with an exquisite Viré-Clessé.

"This is from a small business near Mâcon, Gilles, and Catherine Vergé. They only make wine aged in steel tanks," she explained to him before noticing the white tome resting on the table. "And what is that book?"

"*Merci, ma chérie.* I picked it up just now at the stalls back there." Tommaso proudly displayed the white cover with the red goblet as if he had written it.

"It would look great on that shelf with ours!" Julie pointed to a wrought-iron shelf where different-sized books devoted to the universe of wine, vineyards, flavors, smells, the secrets of perlage, and so on were lined up.

"For now, it will look great on my nightstand. Then we'll see. Speaking of wines, what have you decided for Saturday? Are you with us?"

"Sure, I'm serious about it."

Tommaso knew that when Julie claimed to be serious about her intentions, it meant only one thing, she would be carried out of a club clouded by alcohol fumes or in the throes of uncontrollable laughter. Last time they had struggled considerably to pull her away from a lamppost, to which she had clung, claiming that it was the love of her life.

"Give me your opinion on the wine! I opened it a few hours ago to let it breathe, and it has no added sulfites," Julie continued.

After inhaling intensely, Tommaso took a couple of sips.

"An explosion of medicinal herbs. Fresh and intensely complex. You can detect smoky nuances and ripe fruit, plus it has a good acidic level. Very good structure! I like it, yes!"

"Me too. I find it excellent, and it's definitely outside the box compared to a lot of producers in that area."

"Anyway, Luciano and I had an idea," Tommaso suddenly said.

"What idea? To purchase a vineyard?"

Tommaso did not have time to answer her because someone across the room called Julie's attention back.

"Everyone is leaving soon, don't worry. So you can tell me about it at your leisure," his friend reassured him before walking away.

When she was back about ten minutes later, slightly flushed and with a small glass of wine, Tommaso motioned her to sit next to him. The girl handed him the goblet she held in her hands.

"From the color and smell, you'd think it was a Sangiovese."

"Chapeau! It is a Chianti Classico Riserva from Castello dei Rampolla. It's not pure Sangiovese, but I'll still promote it!" Julie sighed briefly and looked at him with her deep brown eyes. "I love this trade."

"But you are studying to be a physiotherapist..."

"I know," she replied, wrinkling her nose. "What do you want me to say? It will be the lure of the roots. The job in the wine bar was to pay for my studies. I didn't think it would turn into my greatest passion. The idea of becoming a physiotherapist doesn't appeal to me as much as it did when I started college. Still, I'm going to finish it anyway. Then, if all goes well..."

"If all goes well, what will you do?"

"I will open my own wine bar. It will be called *Chez Julie*."

"I suppose your grandparents will be thrilled at your decision."

"Grandpa, yes, because he is a hopeless romantic. Grandma, no, because she has her feet firmly planted on the ground and would probably prefer to see me accomplished in other fields."

"But she..."

"I know, I know," Julie interrupted him, waving her hand in midair, "and that is precisely why she tries to direct me elsewhere. She has dedicated her life to wine, and she has never left her vineyard because Grandpa always went on business trips. Try explaining to her that running a wine bar is not the same thing. She's probably just tired."

Tommaso nodded. He loved the subtle French accent in his friend's perfect Italian. He could have stayed and listened to her talk for hours.

"Let's get back to us," Julie changed the subject, poking a small cube of Parmesan with a toothpick and popping it into her mouth. "What idea did you people have? Not a vineyard, I hope. Otherwise, I'll turn my grandmother against you."

They laughed and took long sips from their respective glasses. Tommaso cleared his throat.

"Are you ready? I'm warning you; it's a real bomb. Do you know Romanée-Conti?" he asked her, showing her his palms as if he were reciting the Lord's Prayer.

"Who doesn't know it! It's one of my forbidden dreams."

"Then I'll tell you, Romanée-Conti from 1991."

"I can't remember by heart if it's one of the best vintage wines, but it's certainly very expensive, and I'd be dying to drink one! So?"

"I thought we'd take up some kind of collection among ourselves and give each other a bottle. I've talked to Luciano about it, he isn't convinced yet, but I'm working on it. Then, on Saturday, we'll tell Roberta and-"

"Tom..." Julie was looking at him as if he were twelve years old.

"Tell me."

"A bottle of 1991 Romanée-Conti will cost at least fifteen thousand euros! Granted, I'm not someone who's particularly attached to money, but I'm certainly not swimming in gold, and, as far as I know, neither are you. You've just opened a law firm, and Luciano is getting a divorce. He has a twenty-year-old daughter with her own needs, plus a new partner..."

"We found a good offer. Twelve thousand euros, and there's plenty of time to..."

Julie burst out laughing.

"Tom, I knew you were out of your mind, but I didn't think to this extent. Does 12,000 euros for a bottle of wine sound like a bargain to you?"

He emptied his glass, stood up to pay, and got in line behind a couple of young American tourists waiting at the counter. He looked outside to the streets were full of busy people. A line of seagulls passed between buildings looking for a few bags of garbage to bash through.

That gutted me. Admittedly, I think this Romanée-Conti idea is just bullshit.

CHAPTER 4

*"I love everything that is old; old friends, old times, old manners, old books, old
wines."*
Oliver Goldsmith

Being an avid lover of walking along the city center
streets, Tommaso reached Campo de' Fiori on foot shortly
before seven o'clock. Giordano Bruno, the Italian
philosopher, stood on his pedestal, reflecting as if
crystallizing an insistent thought, an unsolvable enigma.

Perhaps he was meditating on miserable human
conditions, the hopeless ignorance that slays philosophers
and exalts bloodthirsty monsters.

At that hour of the day, one could still see a deep blue,
almost violet light in the sky above the buildings. It looked
as if a giant fried egg had exploded on a frying pan of
immense size. Yellow dripped between clusters of pearl-
gray clouds, some still white despite dusk, and scalloped
their contours, making them look like gold.

Tommaso noticed the woman getting out of the cab on
the other side of the street.

"Hey, Roberta. Over here!"

"Tommy!"

When she came over to him, she placed two kisses on
his cheeks. As usual, she had not gone lightly. She smelled
and sparkled like an actress, ready to walk the red carpet.

"Oh my!! You look beautiful!"

"It's Saturday night, honey. At least once a week, a
woman should be able to indulge in a few luxuries. I guess
I overdid it with the Chanel, though. At one point, the taxi
driver rolled down all the windows!"

As they headed toward Via dei Banchi Vecchi, Roberta took the opportunity to catch up on her friend's situation.

"Since we're still sober, tell me a little about how you're doing. Is the studio giving you any satisfaction?"

"Everything is going pretty well. The new firm is off to a great start: great clients, and business looks promising. There's been a bit of a rift with Piergiorgio, but I think that's normal."

"Your shark partner?"

"That's the one. We have quite different personalities and somewhat different interpretations of ethics, and we still have to find a balance."

"Don't let him run you down."

"No, that's not it. You know how stubborn I am. However, I must confess he has some annoying habits, and I sometimes want to kill him. As for me, maybe I should open up a little more and be able to be less meticulous and analytical if you know what I mean. Less logical sometimes. Maybe that would help."

"Partnerships help build character, my dear," said Roberta, dishing out some of her protective affection that Tommaso had long since grown accustomed to. At fifty-two, with a seemingly endless amount of energy that matched an enviable physique and a marked propensity for irony, Roberta was a bit like an auntie, always ready to give advice and pearls of wisdom, as well as being an extremely pleasant and entertaining trouper.

"Here's a story. About fifteen years ago, I ran a very small art gallery with a partner. I discovered that she was withholding information from me to keep the contacts of big collectors to herself. Eventually, I beat her up."

"You beat her up?!"

"You got it right. When I found out what she was doing, I beat her up good..."

" Thereby sanctioning the end of a partnership."

" Plus, I broke her nose."

Luciano and Julie were waiting for them in front of the Grand Cru wine bar. They were absorbed in reading the menu framed in a display case hanging next to the front door.

"Do they have enough wines for our very refined palates?" asked Tommaso peeking over Luciano's shoulder. He shook his hand and kissed Julie on the cheek.

"They have about three hundred," exclaimed the girl as she pulled Roberta into a brief embrace. "We'll get enough for tonight."

Five minutes later, they were all seated around a carefully set wooden table, busy perusing the wine list.

"Instead of going to our French cousins for Champagne as usual, I suggest we start with a Trento DOC."

Luciano's suggestion garnered everyone's approval. When the four appetizers arrived, the table was filled with color and fragrance. After presenting a bottle of Maso Martis' Extra Brut Riserva Rosé, the waiter proceeded to pour the wine. The four friends particularly appreciated the perlage (effervescence) and great structure of the wine.

"Years ago," Roberta suddenly revealed, "I started writing short stories dedicated to wine, but then I didn't continue."

"Really?" exclaimed Luciano, surprised. "I didn't know, so why don't you let us read them?"

"No way. I should find them again first and then fix them. I wrote them a long time ago."

"You could update them and put us in as the characters," said Tommaso.

"Guys, I think you are overestimating me. These were things without any ambition. Besides, what would be so interesting about our raids between wineries and restaurants that we could inspire new stories?"

Tommaso exchanged an understanding look with Luciano.

"To be honest," he interjected, "there might even be something great to put in a book about the four of us."

"Oh yeah?" asked Roberta, amused.

"Aaah!" inserted Julie as she raised her goblet, "Now that I remember, someone has to make a big proposal tonight. Am I right, Tom?"

"I hope it's not an obscene proposal since I'm married," joked her friend.

Julie burst out laughing, then lent Tommaso a helping hand.

"I know what it's about, but only vaguely, and I'd like our dear friend to explain to everyone the latest folly he has hatched. Go ahead and speak..."

"How about I start telling you what it's all about, and if it goes bad, you'll step in as my lawyer," said Luciano, who had returned to his friend's proposal in the previous twenty-four hours, no longer finding it so absurd. The expense was considerable, but it was for a passion they shared. After all, it would be a memorable way to toast their friendship. After a nod of agreement from Tommaso, he began his speech.

"You know those things that one does only once in a lifetime? Those things that you can only do between true friends, and then you remember them forever, and when you're old, you tell your grandchildren about them on Christmas night?"

"Mh-mh," Roberta encouraged him to continue, refilling her glass again.

"We all love wine more than we love our partners," Luciano began again. With a divorce in place and a new relationship riddled with messiness, he was definitely believable for that kind of statement. "Wouldn't it be wonderful, for once, to treat ourselves to a trip to heaven and drink the sort of bottle that, in an entire existence, only happens once?"

The attentive silence at the table confirmed Tommaso's belief that his friend had hit the nail on the head.

"That's why Tommaso and I thought of suggesting that we all pitch in and try to buy a Romanée-Conti to drink together, in cheer, raising a glass to our beautiful friendship."

"That doesn't sound so crazy to me," Roberta interrupted him before nibbling on a shrimp sprinkled with a flavored sauce. "What bottle did you think of? An Échezeaux? Or maybe a Corton?"

"No, no!" Julie exclaimed. "They really have Romanée-Conti[1] in mind. From 1991, to be precise." Roberta choked, possibly on an olive, a crust of bread, or more likely when she heard 1991. The fact was that she began to cough, and Luciano, who was sitting next to her, had to pat her back as one does with children until she recovered.

---

[1] Domaine de la *Romanée-Conti*, an iconic winery in Burgundy wine country, produces several wines. They are all expensive and sought-after, the best known and rarest of which is called *Romanée-Conti*, after the vineyard itself.

"Do you get it now?" continued Julie in satisfaction. "Oh, so they found a bargain for only twelve thousand euros. Let's get it for next Saturday. We can celebrate an early New Year's Eve and then go see a shrink!"

Roberta took a sip of wine, trying to calm herself down.

"Guys, I have to admit that out of all the crap I've ever heard in my life, this goes straight to the podium. Congratulations!"

"Come on, don't be so crushing," Luciano resumed after finishing his wine. "After all, it would be precisely one of those things that... and you, a lawyer, would like to come to my rescue, or have you decided just to stand there and dream about that bottle for the rest of your life? And to say that the idea came from you!"

Tommaso shook himself. He had to laugh. After all, he was a lawyer and knew his trade well. But this was an evening with friends, and the alcohol inside him had spread a veil of indefinable, almost poetic, lightness that inhibited his logical and pragmatic side in favor of the chatty and buffoonish one. Before speaking, he cleared his throat.

"Dear friends, do you or do you not want to drink a glass of great wine at least once in your life? I do, and Luciano does too. Look, we are not asking you to sell your house or car or take out a mortgage tomorrow morning. We are going to figure it out. Make some plans. Otherwise, what adventure about wine friends would you put in the book?"

For the second time that evening, silence fell around the table. Then Julie began to consider the whole matter aloud.

"I am a student who, as you know, makes a living sweating it out at the wine bar, but I do have a little something saved up. I absolutely love to drink and drink well and wisely, together with the right people. The right people, for me, are you. I'm also not one to go out of my way to offer and to spend. So, if we're going to invest a lot of money, let's do it right. I'm in for fifty percent. That means that before you have the remaining fifty, you will have to explain to me in full how you intend to raise twelve thousand euros to buy the bottle."

Luciano applauded. Roberta looked at her admiringly.

"You know what?" intervened the woman, who, in the meantime, had returned to perusing the restaurant's enormous wine list. "I think it's time to order a nice Rhine Riesling and have the entrees come in. For example, they have a 2008 Silberlack from Schloss Johannisberg. Or perhaps you would prefer something else? Maybe a Burgundy?"

"Let's go for Riesling," Luciano approved.

Again, no one had any objections, and Roberta called the waiter to order.

"'You know what? I'm in, too,'" she added as soon as the waiter had departed. "The gallery is doing a little worse than I'm used to as they're cutting funding for the arts. I'm certainly not swimming in gold, you know. Oh, and Mario still has a mortgage payment. However, as luck would have it, I managed to close a pretty good deal just a few days ago, so screw it. I'm in! If we can scrape together all the money, as long as you don't propose we rob a bank, I assure you I'm in."

A new round of applause followed.

"It's a lot of money, though," she added.

"True. But the central issue is not thinking you can do it. Getting it done. All together!" Tommaso's enthusiasm was through the roof.

"It's not like it's a sports competition," Roberta commented, "but I see what you mean. Tagliatelle with porcini mushrooms for everyone?"

"For me, cacio e pepe," replied Tommaso.

"For me, carbonara," Luciano added a second later.

"Aren't you on a diet?"

"Not today, Julie. Not today."

At that moment, the wine finally arrived at the table.

Roberta was instructed to sample it while the others waited for her response in religious silence. As soon as the waiter had finished filling the glasses, Julie resumed the conversation.

"Today, we celebrate the beginning of our great adventure to conquer the Romanée-Conti of 1991!"

"Now that we all agree," Luciano said after the toast, "let us have a few days to plan our spending. By next Saturday, we will have the plan in all its magnificence."

"Cheers!" exclaimed Roberta, raising her glass again.

"To Romanée-Conti '91!" echoed Julie, and the clinking of glasses sparkled almost as much as their eyes.

CHAPTER 5

Tommaso flung open the windows through which he could see the green and yellow foliage of the Plane trees and inhaled smog mixed with the scent of fried doughnuts. That morning, Piergiorgio had a session in court and was not going to stop by the studio. So he rang the café downstairs and ordered a second breakfast to be delivered. It was still Monday, after all, and it was the Monday after the big proposal to the group.

He was not convinced that Roberta's and Julie's "half-hearted no" would actually become a yes. Even if they planned for the expense, they would still have to pay a considerable sum of money up front to try to match the final amount, and none of them were rich.

Besides, Luciano raised an objection from the very first moment. If each person found three, four, or five thousand euros to spend within a few days, would the wisest thing really be to invest it in a bottle of wine? It would have turned out to be a magnificent ephemeral joy destined to fade away in four glasses of absolute pleasure or a mad bliss that would have snatched away care and opportunity from other people. He was single and childless, but what about Luciano? After his divorce, he really wanted to gift his daughter a trip to Japan. She had dreamed of it since she was a little girl. With that amount of money, Roberta would have been able to fix up the old apartment she lived in. Julie would have paid for her college education until she graduated.

Priorities, pondered Tommaso. *Life is all about priorities. Yet, even stepping into the economic needs of a family, I still struggle to rank what is most important. Ethically speaking, if a person has children, their needs come first. It is unfair, but that is how it is. Where do we put personal satisfaction, though?*

The doorbell rang, stirring him from those thoughts. He was not expecting customers, and the delivery guy would have had to fly to be there already. He hurried to open the door.

"Tommaso Mariani, right?"

"Yes..."

The beautiful girl in a gray suit smiling at him on the landing was Sara Altini, a brilliant lawyer from a prestigious firm Piergiorgio worked with from time to time. Although he had never spoken to her, she had certainly not gone unnoticed by Tommaso among the many colleagues he had seen in court. Based on a couple of glances of understanding exchanged quickly on his way out of the courtroom, he had hoped, in turn, that she had noticed him.

"Yes, that's me," he confirmed after a moment.

"Sara Altini, nice to meet you. I have often seen you in court, but until recently, I did not know about your new firm with lawyer Pizzi. Congratulations!"

They shook hands. Tommaso, embarrassed, invited her in.

"We still have boxes of books around," he justified himself, realizing even more at that moment how empty and bare the studio was. "We're still settling in."

"My partners told me this morning," she continued, " they had to pass some papers to Pizzi, so I decided to drop by. Is Piergiorgio here?"

"No, he's in court. Would you like a coffee?"

"Oh no, thank you. I've already had two, and it's not even ten o'clock. Wow! What a beautiful setting!"

She's lying, and she knows it, Tommaso told himself as he led the way through the apartment. He had always had a soft spot for the girl, but she was certainly not the type to make a move. Besides, she could be married. Instinctively he looked at her hands. No wedding ring, just a little gold ring with a tiny diamond.

She's engaged, he deduced despondently, as she placed a pack of papers in his cold hands.

"Here, could you do me a favor and give these papers to Pizzi?"

She smiled at him, and Tommaso thought she had the most beautiful smile in the world.

"Now that you are in business with Piergiorgio, we will probably see a lot of each other," she added. "Maybe, one day, I'll invite you to lunch."

"Why not?"

Make no mistake, Tommy, these are things that are said between colleagues. She will actually disappear into thin air, and if you meet her on the street, she will pretend she doesn't know you.

"What is that? Are you into wine?"

Tommaso followed the trajectory of Sara's finger and glimpsed the Wine Encyclopedia he had bought the week before and forgotten to take home. Perhaps it had been no accident. That book exuded color and joy. Not only did it talk about wine on a technical level, but it was also about sharing beautiful things. Keeping it in the studio made the environment a bit like home.

"Yes, here it is," he replied, handing the book to her. She flipped through it carefully.

"It is a genuine world," commented Sara after a few seconds. "Much more than a pastime, isn't it? As far as I know, those who love wine are ultimately also deep connoisseurs of gastronomy and culinary delights."

"It's true. Those things go together quite well," Tommaso admitted. "I got into wine tasting a few years ago almost by accident. Then I took some sommelier courses, and, you know, one thing led to another."

"I really admire you."

Sara smiled again, making Tommaso blush. "I'm all about home and study. I take my work home and spend my weekends rereading cases and sifting through documents."

Was it an invitation to ask her out? Tommaso blushed again.

"Are you kidding? A girl like you, locked in the house studying all the time? What a waste!"

He laughed nervously. Luckily, she joined him.

I might ask her to come with me next Saturday, but what if she says no? I will have a working relationship with her, so I can't hit on her right away. I would risk blowing the whole thing.

"Do you drink very expensive wines, or has your experience led you to appreciate ordinary yet special wines?" asked Sara.

Good question. You are the woman of my life.

"I generally drink wines that I can afford without making too many sacrifices," replied Tommaso, scratching the back of his head. "However, together with my group of friends, we are about to do something crazy."

"Meaning?" urged Sara, lighting up like a star.

"We decided to buy a bottle of 1991 Romanée-Conti to have the drink of a lifetime in honor of friendship and living life to the full!" he proclaimed, marveling at the passion with which he had uttered that sentence.

"Judging by how you talk about it, it sounds like an expensive wine."

"Not only that, it is probably the most famous wine in the world!"

"If so, my admiration for you is skyrocketing," Sara said as she headed for the door. "Life is not all about work and career, but it is not easy to realize it. Eventually, we get overwhelmed by our inescapable commitments and forget about ourselves. You, however, are alive, and outside your office, you have a world that most people dream about. Way to go, Tom. May I call you Tom?"

You can call me anything.

"Certainly. And thank you, I never realized I was so lucky. Now, though, I do."

"It's not luck," she retorted as she stepped out onto the landing and tied her hair in a ponytail with a black rubber band. "I'd say it's the ability, combined with the will, to enjoy life. Nothing falls from the sky, Tom. Have a good day!"

He saw her running down the stairs and did not even have time to say "goodbye." However, she was not quick enough to keep him from noticing the hint of sadness that flashed in her eyes for a moment.

CHAPTER 6

"Wine resembles a man. It will never be known to what extent it can be
estimated or despised, loved or hated nor of what sublime deeds
or monstrous misdeeds it is capable of."
Charles Baudelaire

Tommaso got home late after a long day of work and in the pouring rain. The month of October always made the city of Rome look spectacular due to the weather and fall colors. That time, it seemed strange.

Perhaps I'm not a kid anymore, and the sheer weight of things exhausts me well before I can grasp their beauty, he thought as he slipped into his pajamas, shivering in the freezing house.

Or, more simply, I got tired of being single and focusing on my career, and I'm starting to feel lonely.

He looked around and switched on the lamps in the small living room. He picked a couple of books from the shelf above the fireplace and laid them on the sofa, along with an IKEA plaid blanket. He went into the kitchen intending to make himself a hot cup of coffee but ultimately decided to have tea.

'Oh dear, am I so old that I make tea in the evening?'

That thought cracked a smile on his face. Ever since he opened the firm, the weeks seemed to be getting shorter and shorter. Sometimes he would stay glued to his desk past dinnertime, thumbing through papers and going over long litigation court cases, forgetting sacred things like friends and food, and most importantly, wine.

If succeeding as a lawyer means giving up the few pleasures life offers, I doubt it's really worth it.

Sipping his tea, he stood for a few minutes watching the rain draw twisted strokes on the glass and, up ahead, the old yellowed willows in the courtyard tossed in the wind. He suddenly grabbed his smartphone and called Julie.

"Hey!"

He could barely hear his friend's voice through a background of indistinct sounds. Tommaso smacked his hand on his forehead.

"Oh my goodness, are you still working? Sorry, I didn't think about that!"

"No, Tommy, don't worry! It's my night off, and I'm at a birthday party in Testaccio. It's a nice place, but they serve non-alcoholic beer. So, send help!"

Tommaso felt relieved. On that rainy evening, Julie's voice was a ray of sunshine.

"If I weren't exhausted, I'd suggest we meet downtown for drinks. I can't imagine you with a glass of non-alcoholic beer."

"Don't worry. I've now succumbed to my fate. You know, Tommy, to be honest, it's times like these that I feel I have to do something pretty epic, something like...."

The music in the background grew deafening and, for a few seconds, muffled the girl's voice. Then the decibel overdose became a buzz mixed with the sound of the wind.

"I came out to the balcony. At least out here, you can breathe and talk."

"Something epic, you said."

"Yes, something to add meaning to my day-to-day life, to make me feel alive, outside of the wine bar, which I also love, and university. A great adventure, one of those things that prove to you that you're really living."

Julie's enthusiasm, so far removed from the vague "I would, if..." to which he used to relegate his dreams that seemed too big to be realized, made him feel even more trapped within his mental chains as a young lawyer on the rise. Only then did he understand why the idea of the bottle, just as concrete and definite, had managed to make its way into his thoughts and those of his friends. It may not have been the epic adventure Julie had in mind, but it was a challenge he could approach and was definitely the path for him to break out of the stalemate that threatened to extinguish him little by little.

"Hey, did you fall asleep? I guess I knocked you out with my ramblings."

"On the contrary, Julie, I was mulling over your last words. They were so strong and pure. I just needed that tonight."

"You needed to hear crazy things coming from a girl with a glass of who-knows-what in her hand?"

"Exactly."

"Then you did the right thing by calling me. By the way, where are we going on Saturday? We need a quiet place so we can plan the drink of the century."

"I have no idea. Luciano said he would make a reservation, perhaps..."

"I heard from him a couple of hours ago," Julie interrupted.

"He took his daughter out to dinner, but he's upset because she wanted to go listen to some rapper at some small club in San Lorenzo. Poor Luciano, the divorce is costing him dearly. Well, I have to hang up now. It's deadly cold out here. Good night Tommy!"

"Good night. Enjoy your evening!"

After hanging up, Tommaso replayed his friend's words in his head. It all now appeared in a new perspective. The money and the sacrifices had made way for the dream to be fulfilled together. The delight they would have in sharing such a fine wine made it even more magical by the tale of its origins.

Wine is history, friendship, sharing, roots, origins, flavor, and life.

By indulging in that sudden euphoria, he fell into a deep sleep.

CHAPTER 7

"Wine is sunlight, held together by water."
Galileo Galilei

The ambiance at *Sette Colli*, a long-established restaurant serving regional cuisine near Piazza Navona, was the perfect setting for a delectable dinner. Luciano was the last to arrive.

He was breathless and complained about the traffic. Roberta had a severe cold, and Julie, wearing a short-sleeve dress, seemed imbued with fiery spirits.

They ordered a charcuterie board as a starter, followed by a revised version of Gnocchi Alla Romana (a typical dish at the restaurant), artichokes Alla Romana, codfish, and lamb chops. They decided to go for something local for the wine and ordered two bottles of Cesanese del Piglio.

Tommaso praised the wine's qualities while swirling his glass between his fingers despite Roberta's objection. For dessert, they had a huge maritozzo (a classic sweet bun filled with whipped cream) with melted chocolate on the side to be divided into four equal parts.

"Romanée-Conti, commencing the proceedings," Tommaso broke the lingering hesitation by tapping his teaspoon on the nearly empty second bottle of Cesanese.

"I'm in!" exclaimed Julie immediately.

"I can put seven hundred euros on the table in a week. You?"

"We're on a roll!" replied Luciano jokingly, tossing her a tiny piece of bread amid laughter from the others.

"I'll put in two thousand euros for now," said Tommaso.

Julie clapped her hands.

"If Tommy gives two thousand, I can't fall short, so here it is!" intervened Luciano again, placing a bundle of invisible bills on the table.

"Gee, I was hoping for less, but I'll go along with you." Roberta flapped her napkin, pretending to faint.

"Clearly, this only goes through if we can reach the set amount, as in crowdfunding," Tommaso pointed out.

"Right now, we have six thousand seven hundred euros in hand, and that's more than half of what we need. Good start! If we want to get the bottle we have been eyeing on the website, we have a few weeks left to raise another five thousand three hundred euros. If not, we could try other auctions, but there is no guarantee that the price will be as good. What I'm saying is we must not, by any stretch of the imagination, diminish the significance of this project by resorting to less expensive or less valuable wine. If we can't have the '91 Romanée-Conti, everyone will get their money back, and so be it!"

Tommaso's cheeks were red, and his eyes sparkled.

"Sounds reasonable to me," concurred Roberta. "That's the goal. Let's keep an eye on the website and hope no one outbids us."

Then, lowering her voice and looking her friends one by one in the eye, she added, "By the way, I haven't told my husband any of this, and I don't intend to. By now, he and I have our own lives, interests, and private things. This will be my little secret. So if you happen to meet him, try not to spoil it for me by opening your mouths."

"That's fine with me," nodded Luciano, who had not looked away from Tommaso.

"Nice speech! If you fail as a lawyer, you can always go into politics. Five thousand three hundred euros divided by four makes one thousand three hundred fifty each. We have to come up with the money within two weeks at most, otherwise bye-bye, bottle! Just as we saw it online, many others probably noticed it."

Julie waved the waiter over with her hand and asked for coffee to wrap up the meal.

"I was thinking—since I have a lot of things I no longer need in the attic, I could sort them out and sell them to match your offers without messing up my finances too much. If I have any money left over after that, we could always allocate it to our cause. What do you say?"

"That's a very good idea," Tommaso brightened up.

"I, too, have several things I can sell, including a tablet in mint condition. This way, we could win on every front. We get rid of unnecessary clutter and cash in on something that will really make us happy. How do we move forward? Do we simply get a booth or stall at the *Città della Nuova Economia*?"

Julie's smirk dampened her enthusiasm.

"I hope you're kidding. We're about to buy a bottle online, and you're talking to me about the Sunday market! That is so nineteenth-century!"

"Be good and listen to me," Luciano interrupted them by raising his glass. "Go ahead and set up your flea markets and do your hippie stuff. However, if you can't put in your share, I will pay it up-front so you won't waste too much time. Then you can return the advance to me in your own time."

"If they can't raise their dues right away, you and I will pay it up-front, half each, because you have a family," Roberta corrected him, emphasizing the last part of her sentence and making everyone laugh.

"Actually, I have to tell you a secret," Luciano shot back, turning to his friends schemingly." I have not told Monica about our project either. She's already trying to take everything from me with the divorce—even my underwear. Imagine what a freaking mess she'd make if she found out about our stunt! Also, I didn't say anything to Victoria. What would she think of me if she knew I was so spoiled? Obviously, I didn't say anything to Catherine either because that woman would report me to social services right away regarding the trip to Japan.

Oh, and what a drag this trip to Japan is! First, the Erasmus study abroad program, then the O-Bag, then the newest iPhone... I don't know whether I have a daughter or a human leech!"

"Shut up!" rebutted Roberta affectionately, tossing him a napkin.

"All right," Tommaso concluded. "I think we're all set!"

CHAPTER 8

"Wine is one of the most civilized things in the world"
Ernest Hemingway

In a pastry shop on Via del Corso, Julie and Tommaso were intent on making a list of possible items to sell online over two hot chocolates with cream. Beyond the shop windows, crowds of chattering tourists and Romans huddled in their windbreakers walked briskly toward who knows where. Every now and then, a gust of wind carried swarms of brown leaves that, for a moment, hid the world from the view of the two friends, then settled like tired butterflies on the sidewalk.

"After all, that's the beauty of it, isn't it?" she observed, taking a spoonful of cream and bringing it to her mouth.

"What would that be exactly?" asked Tommaso, briefly lifting his eyes from his list.

"Spending time together. I mean, I think there is more to what we're doing than simply buying a bottle of wine, no matter how fancy. All right, I get the ecstatic experience, I get the taste, but in the end, it's also a way to celebrate our friendship, right? Even the way we decided to raise the money, I find it a fun pastime. Plus, it's useful because we clean up our houses and get rid of all those things we no longer use. In the end, money comes and goes. It doesn't matter in life. What's left is the people we enjoy it with, right?"

"You and Luciano have been more poetic than usual lately. What's going on? He's in love, but what's up with you?"

"I'm just reflecting on life. Does it seem that strange to you?"

Tommaso took another sip of his chocolate, careful not to get cream on his nose.

"I'm just kidding. No offense. The same thoughts have been on my mind since we came up with this idea."

"By the way, I asked my grandparents if I could get my Christmas present early. I want to match the amount you and the others are putting in. I don't like the idea of owing you guys." Julie said, changing the subject.

"Do they usually write you a check?"

"Bank transfer. Christmas is Christmas, and I'm their only grandchild."

"But it's October! You have some nerve."

"October, November—what difference does it make? Come on, help me write this ad!"

"Okay, but let's make it quick because I have to run to the office in five minutes."

***

Sara was a sun capable of brightening his gray days, and Tommaso was happy that their respective firms were on good terms. Due to the continuous exchange of documents and information, he often managed to see or speak to her.

So he was not surprised when, on a late and unusually cold afternoon, Sara invited him for coffee (even though they had no work papers to exchange). At the end of a brief phone call, speaking a little faster than usual, she had asked him how busy he was.

"Right now, I'm not that busy," he had replied. Five minutes later, he was already running down the driveway toward the bus stop, under the dim light of street lamps, dodging the first fiery red leaves that fell from the maple trees.

A few blocks away, near the old town, Sara was waiting for him, sitting at a wrought-iron table in a small French-style bistro. She had ditched her discreet office attire in favor of a pleated skirt in fall colors that went down to mid-legs, worn over heavy stockings. She also wore a white blouse, a camel-colored cape matching the skirt, a string of pearls around her neck, and a mustard-colored beret, looking like a Parisian tourist who had got lost through the city streets.

She was so beautiful and colorful that, in Tommaso's eyes, she appeared like a modern-day Little Red Riding Hood surrounded by a forest of buildings and lights. She smiled at him as soon as she saw him emerge from around the street corner. At that very moment, Tommaso realized that standing before him was the authentic version of his ideal girl. That revelation made him euphoric.

"Hi, Sara. Sorry, I'm late!"

"Actually, you're early."

While exchanging the customary kisses in greeting her, Tommaso felt her perfume hit him like a whiff of spring air that radiated a feeling of well-being. A moment later, an icy gust of wind lifted his gray overcoat, making him feel a little out of place next to her simple beauty.

"I like your outfit. It's so..." he exclaimed, incapable of completing the sentence.

What exactly was he going to say? Vintage? Retro? Elegantly poetic? She intervened and got him off the hook.

"Thank you! I was at the office earlier, reviewing some case files, when I decided to reward myself for the last few weeks of hard work by going for a walk. I stopped by my place to change and thought I'd invite you to meet for a snack. How are you, Tom?"

There she is, the real Sara. Out of the conventional fabric dictated by social rules. Who determined that lawyers should always be gray and boring? Tommaso smiled as he heard her utter the word "snack." For a moment, he imagined what the whole picture would have looked like if he, too, had stopped by the house to change, perhaps wearing jeans, a shirt, and that checkered vest that made him feel so *bohemian*.

"I'm fine. Can't complain. Not everything I've planned recently is going great, but there aren't any catastrophes either. So I'm content. Besides, I'm having a snack with you, so I'd say it's all good!"

"You've been looking tired lately, and I wanted to make sure everything was okay. Your partner must not be easy to work with."

"We shouldn't talk about work over snacks," he deflected.

The waitress approached them, carrying an electronic notebook, and took their order while Tommaso wondered if they still used pencil and paper in Montmartre. A few minutes later, she brought apple pie and a lemon-and-ginger herbal tea for Sara and American coffee for him.

"It's been ages since I took some time for myself after work, and I even went shopping," Sara revealed. Showing him shopping bags of various sizes from different stores in the area. For no particular reason, that news gave him intense pleasure.

"What about you? How do you spend your free time? You mentioned you have many friends..."

Maybe you are not engaged after all, thought Tommaso. *Perhaps you really do divide all your time between the law firm and home. But what am I thinking? Such a beautiful and intelligent woman surely has a whole court of suitors waiting for the right moment to ask her out. I am her snack friend.*

"I have a small group of friends. We have a lot in common; we're quiet people who enjoy eating and drinking well. I also like to read, mostly before I go to sleep. I prefer technical topics, but I also enjoy other genres."

"What do you mean by technical?"

Whenever she spoke, she leaned forward, slightly tilting her face to the side, as one does when they are very interested in something—or someone.

"I'm into photography."

"Wow! I know almost nothing about it, but I've always been fascinated by the world of images."

Tommaso imagined taking pictures of her on a Sunday afternoon out of town, maybe at the Roman castles, the lake, or the sea. He pictured her walking on the beach, laughing, with her hair across her face and the sun's glare making her shine like a star.

"Maybe sometime, you could show me some of your pictures if you'd like," Sara continued, rousing him from his daydreams.

"Sure, I'd be happy to. But I warn you: you'll probably get bored. We are talking about billions of shots of sunsets taken from the Pincian Hill, of churches, and monuments—I must have taken over a thousand pictures of the Colosseum alone at all hours of the day and night. You'll also see many flowers because I'm fond of macro photography, therefore butterflies, insects, spikes..."

"I love it! I thought I would see dozens of portraits of pretty women," she interrupted him jokingly. She accidentally bumped the still half-full cup with her hand, spilling a few drops of herbal tea on her skirt. "What a mess! I'm so clumsy!" she said, playfully scolding herself as she blushed.

"What are you talking about? Besides, maybe I can teach you. Taking pictures develops the inner eye and..."

Sara got a notification on her phone that made him lose his train of thought (assuming he had one). As soon as Sara laid eyes on the display, she sprang to her feet.

"It's very late!" she exclaimed.

She reached for her wallet, but he signaled her to stop, waving his hand.

"Forgive me, Tommaso. Time flies. I really have to get going. Thanks for everything, for the great company—I promise I'll make it up to you."

In a matter of seconds, Tommaso found himself standing alone in the cold, silent avenue that had suddenly lost all its magic. He paid the bill and walked away in the direction opposite to the one in which Sara had vanished running. The few certainties he thought he had gained about that mysterious girl had crumbled, and their meeting only left him with endless unanswered questions cluttering his mind.

He went back home feeling down in the dumps. He liked Sara. He was not simply infatuated. Besides being delicate and feminine, she was smart and had a strong personality.

He would have liked to introduce her to Julie, Luciano, and Roberta, but he was afraid to mix those two worlds. He made himself a *club sandwich*, opened a bottle of beer, filled one of his collectible pint glasses, and took a long sip.

"Why did you run away like that, Sara?" he wondered aloud.

The sound of his voice felt strange inside the tidy kitchen, where everything had a definite place. The mug set upside down to dry above the sink, the cork mat ready on the table for dinner, the coffee pot filled with coffee powder for the following morning, the nearly empty refrigerator, and the pantry overflowing with snacks and canned foods painted the picture of the perfect single man's home—a picture that lately had been looking rather faded to him.

The phone rang.

"Roberta, hi! Yes, I'm home. Is everything all right?"

"Everything is fine, dear. I called to see how you and Julie are doing with your garage sale."

"Great! We've already managed to sell most of what we didn't even remember having."

"Hey, you guys aren't emptying your apartments, are you? Let's keep in mind that we're talking about a bottle of wine. A valuable one for sure, but it's still a whim, okay?"

"Relax, Roby. We're not twelve!" They laughed together. Then the woman prepared to strike him.

"Tell me something..."

"What?"

"Is something going on between you and Juliette?" she asked mischievously.

Tommaso was caught off guard and coughed before answering.

"Excuse me? What makes you think that?"

"Nothing. It's just that you guys look so cute, and you're the youngest in the group. I'd love to see you end up together!"

"Oh, I get it. You're rambling. Julie and I are just friends."

"I see," retorted Roberta, disappointed. "I'll get over it. Too bad! You two would make a nice couple. You're both attractive, young, with common interests..."

For a moment, Tommaso considered Roberta's words and imagined himself preparing a nice fish dinner and opening a bottle of white wine in Julie's company. But a second later, Sara, the princess of the Forum, entered his fantasy, taking his friend's place.

"Why don't we talk about something serious?" he suddenly said.

"Like what?"

"The money for the wine bottle. When you are ready, deposit it on my prepaid card. I sent you the number in the chat this morning."

"You're always thinking about money! I'm not surprised you're single," retorted Roberta, teasing him.

"Our goal right now is the bottle. Nothing but the bottle. Okay?"

"All right, all right! I have to go now as I have to prepare dinner. Are we meeting at the wine shop on Saturday?"

"No, we'll do a tasting in Rione Monti. I'll send you the time and address. Have a good evening, Roby. Thanks for calling."

"Bye, Tommy. Take care."

After he hung up, Tommaso could not help but ponder Roberta's last words. Was his friend really worried about him and the fact that he was still single? He recognized that he would not have minded changing that by letting Sara into his life.

But how can someone like that be available? She undoubtedly has a man. She is certainly not waiting for me.

Absorbed in those thoughts, he absentmindedly opened the bank application on his phone and checked the prepaid card's balance. Luciano had transferred his two thousand euros. Tommaso transferred his share from his account and stood there, watching those little numbers grow before his eyes. In a few days, he and his closest friends would treat themselves to the best gift in the world.

CHAPTER 9

"Wine is not only drunk, it is smelled, observed, tasted,
sipped and... talked about"
Re Edoardo VII

"What do you do all day long attached to your smartphone?" asked Piergiorgio in a somewhat forced, friendly tone as he leaned out the door of his office.

"I check the accounts. If you keep stealing my clients, at this rate, I'll go bankrupt and have to look for another partner," Tommaso had the promptness to retort. Albeit in a light and deliberately ironic way, he finally managed to get that off his chest. That unpleasant feeling had been nagging him for a couple of months now.

"I only do what's good for the firm," retorted the senior partner defensively. "Where I see shortcomings, I fix them, Tommaso. I am not reprimanding you. When I was a young lawyer, I worked at several firms for almost no fee, hoping to actually learn something from a bunch of old lawyers who sent me to get coffee. Then again, what do you know about starting from the bottom and working your way up? What do you know?"

"In this case, though, the firm is half mine," objected Tommaso, smiling without taking his eyes off the smartphone screen. "I'd rather you tell me what I'm doing wrong than see you close cases I was working on. How else can I learn the business?"

The phone rang, easing them both out of that unpleasant but much-needed conversation. Piergiorgio went back to his office to answer it.

Tommaso logged back into the account and checked the balance on the prepaid card. Julie had deposited one thousand eight hundred euros, and Luciano had already added the missing portion. He whistled lightly so as not to vex Piergiorgio. Then he transferred the entire profit made from online sales, and the result left him ecstatic: twelve thousand euros, raised in three weeks. He took the screenshot and posted it in the group chat, sparking great enthusiasm among his friends.

"See you tomorrow night at the tasting in Monti to buy the bottle and celebrate!"

"Isn't it better to buy it now?" suggested Roberta.

"Have you checked if it's still available?" said Julie.

"It was there this morning," replied Luciano a second later.

Reassured by his friend's words, Tommaso put away his smartphone. A minute later, he reconsidered and decided to secure the bottle right away. If he could get it in twenty-four hours, he would give the others a memorable surprise. The next day, at dinner, they would have been drinking a Romanée-Conti wine aged for more than twenty years!

He inhaled deeply. That moment was sacred, and he certainly would not allow Piergiorgio and his sinister bitterness to ruin it for him. He instinctively grabbed his jacket and hurriedly took the stairs, reaching the building's exit in a matter of seconds. He chose one of the small outdoor bistros near the office where he used to go. As soon as he was seated, he noticed one of his favorites on the menu, Bruno Paillard's Première Cuvée. He immediately ordered a glass. While waiting to be served, he bided his time by consulting the wine list. As soon as the glass arrived at the table, he grabbed his smartphone, entered the auction site, and checked his cart. His bottle was still available.

He took a sip of Champagne following a strange improvised ritual. Then he typed in the prepaid card details, filled in the shipping information, and finally, while holding his breath, clicked on the green button.

He waited for the purchase confirmation. However, after a longer-than-expected loading time, the screen suddenly turned gray, and the words "item not available" appeared.

"What?" he exclaimed as he stood up. "That's not possible! It was there a minute ago..."

He reloaded the page, and the shopping cart was now empty.

He went back to the search page and typed in the name of the bottle again. It was no longer there.

Tommaso slammed the smartphone down on the metal coffee table. The jolt caused the Champagne to spill, and some of it got on his pants.

Calm down, Tommaso. It's probably a connection problem, or maybe I simply mistyped the name.

He turned off the phone and restarted it. He stood still, waiting for the screen to work, watching the app icons reappear one after another. He then opened the search engine again and pulled up the site. As soon as the page refreshed, he slowly typed "Romanée-Conti 1991" in the search box. The hourglass rotated not once, not twice, but thrice and yet the result was the same: article unavailable.

"I can't believe it. What do I tell the others now?" He wondered aloud.

He quickly finished his glass of champagne, paid, and shoved his phone into his jacket pocket. An icy gust of wind hit him in the face, accentuating the feeling of failure that gripped him as swirls of fallen leaves danced in front of him like enormous, beautiful, dusty yellow and gold curtains. He discarded the idea of sharing what happened in the group chat. He decided to cancel the wine tasting at Rione Monti because it would be too chaotic to break the bad news to his friends over there. A quiet dinner at a more secluded trattoria would undoubtedly be better.

Tommaso got off the bus in front of the office building. He pulled out a bunch of keys from his coat, but the glass door swung open in front of him, sweeping him with a pleasant light fragrance.

"Hello, Tommaso! I just asked Piergiorgio about you a moment ago, and here you are!"

Sara's smile, wrapped in a neat blue suit with a coat, blue scarf, and a matching blue cap, was decidedly different from the one with which she had greeted him at the bistro a few days earlier.

Since when did it become Tommaso and not Tom?

"Hi Sara!" he replied, trying not to let the disappointment show. "Are you in for a coffee, or are you in a hurry? Looking at you, I get the feeling that Piergiorgio must have terrified you. You look a little pale..."

To get over the embarrassment, cracking a joke might have proved a winning move, or at least it would have helped break that formal detachment imposed by roles that, after having a snack together, seemed to him at least out of place.

"No thanks, I have to get back to the office right away. I have a client in half an hour. Maybe a rain check?"

Tommaso crossed the threshold, and Sara descended the step that separated her from the sidewalk. Neither of them tried to move away.

Although he quivered with the desire to know why she had left in such a hurry during their afternoon snack, any alternative reason would have helped his suspicion about the boyfriend waiting for her at home. He did not dare to ask her that question. Having to cope with two pieces of bad news in one day would have been too much for Tommaso to handle.

"It will be for the next meeting with my partner," he said simply.

The scent of violets and wisteria became more intense as Sara stepped closer and whispered in his ear.

"Would you be shocked if I told you that your partner is a real dirtbag?"

They both burst out laughing, and Tommaso finally felt the embarrassment melt away.

"I'll let you go now," she said, quickly snapping a hasty kiss on his beard before looking him in the eye and asking him point-blank.
"By the way, did you manage to get that renowned wine you told me about?"

As he told her about the mishap they had run into, Tommaso tried to hide the deep sense of loss he felt. In an attempt to save face, he pointed out that they would still buy the wine—they just had to find another way. He felt like an idiot incapable of even completing an online purchase.

"I'm sure it will all work out in the end, and you'll be able to buy that bottle!" she encouraged him, skipping down the sidewalk.

They said their goodbyes, and Tommaso walked back into the office with the temptation to bang his head against the drywall. He only refrained for fear of smashing through it and landing in Piergiorgio's office with his face covered in rubble.

No Romanée-Conti and no Sara. He turned on his laptop and slumped into the faux-leather armchair he had bought on sale at a department store in the Roman suburbs.

CHAPTER 10

"Now I understand why you decided to cancel the tasting in Rione Monti at the last moment," said Roberta after listening to Tommaso's story. He tried to soften the blow by ordering a bottle of Entre Ciel et Terre by Françoise Bedel, one of his friend's favorite winemakers. He kept his gaze fixed on the bubbles inside his Champagne glass. The small restaurant near the Trevi Fountain he had chosen was cozy and warm. With its beamed ceilings, fireplace, and few rough wooden tables with deliberately mismatched chairs, it looked like a sort of traveler's tavern or retreat for old friends—exactly what they needed that evening.

"This is ridiculous!" exclaimed Julie, shaking her head. "I monitored the bottle until a couple of hours before you attempted to buy it, and I assure you it was there. I'm really sorry, Tommy, but it's not your fault, so get that sad look off your face right now."

"I was looking forward to having an epic drink tonight to celebrate our bottle," snorted Luciano. "Just imagine that to come prepared, I've been on a diet of mineral water and fruit juice all week. Come on, pour me some more Champagne, my friend."

After taking a sip of wine, he began to draw his own conclusions about what had happened.

"Whatever, guys. In the end, it was just a crazy idea. We tried. I'll tell you right now, don't even ask me to invest in some other bottle of wine because I would not participate in the purchase. I was in because it was about that bottle. I'm not interested in any other. With that sum of money, I can take my daughter to Japan. Maybe she jinxed me without even knowing it, that little witch!"

"I agree," Roberta echoed while taking a piece of bread from the basket. "In the end, we put aside some money that might always come in handy."

"But..." objected Tommaso, finally lifting his gaze from the goblet and removing his glasses. "We are not the kind of people who simply give up, are we?"

"What do you mean?" asked Luciano.

"Do you really think that after canceling the scheduled tasting to give you the bad news, I would end the evening on such a sour note? What do you take me for?"

"Are you saying you have a backup plan?" Roberta suddenly rejoiced.

Julie's eyes also lit up. She did not need to say a word to confirm that she was ready to listen with extreme interest to what her friend had to say.

"Listen up," Tommaso continued, "because what I'm about to suggest is not for the faint of heart. In the meantime, I would order a plate of *Cacio e pepe*."

"Forget the *Cacio e pepe* and tell us your idea!" urged Roberta.

"We want to know everything, every last detail," Luciano recoiled, and finally, everyone fell silent.

At that moment, the waitress arrived with the appetizers, giving Tommaso a few extra seconds to find the right words.

Now that he created anticipation and had their undivided attention, he could not make any mistakes. The stakes were too high.

"This might sound a little crazy, but it's really cool," he announced. "Yesterday, I couldn't find peace after missing our chance, so I did thorough online research and finally came across a particularly interesting auction. One of the bottles for sale is a 1991 Romanée-Conti."

He paused to observe his friends' expressions. Everything was going in the best possible way.

"I didn't want to miss such a valuable opportunity, and since the auction had a limited number of participants and there were only a few spots left, I signed up. Clearly, if you're not on board, I can withdraw my registration right away. However, I must tell you that the bottle label is slightly damaged, and that detail might put off more than one wealthy and fierce overseas collector, meaning there is a good chance that the final bidding price will not be much higher than the starting price!"

He paused again, this time to further increase curiosity at the table. Then, he got to the point.

"Bidding starts at nine thousand euros. We have twelve thousand, which might even become more over the next few days, thanks to the garage sale Julie and I have set up. There are still items that have not been purchased. I'd say that bottle is ours!"

"The auction is online, right?" Luciano asked him point blank.

It was the worst question he could have asked.

"Actually, it's an on-site auction. Of course, we could participate remotely, I've looked into it, but it's definitely better to go in person."

"And where does it take place?" asked Julie.

"At *Christie's*. In London." Replied Tommaso, sporting the smile of a child caught doing something naughty.

All hell broke loose at the table.

"I almost believed it. It's cruel to play tricks like that on people, you know?" scolded Roberta, only halfway serious, throwing her napkin in his face.

"You should have told us right away. You let us down!" added Luciano.

Tommaso stood up and waved his hands to shush them.

"Hey, wait a minute! Who said I was joking? It's not like I'm asking you all to go to London. I'll go, get the bottle, and come back."

The protests ceased, but no one spoke to support the project. Tommaso felt the tension rising within him, so he tried to ease it by polishing the lenses of his glasses.

"With a bidding base like that, it will exceed the amount we saved in a moment, and your trip will be completely pointless," Luciano observed, breaking the silence.

"I have a different opinion," Julie suddenly intervened, her eyes twinkling. "I support Tommy's idea, but only partially. I think we should all go to London. It is our project, our dream. That wine can be ours with a little luck and a touch of madness, don't you think? Plus, didn't we say that the whole bottle thing was mostly an opportunity for us to enjoy a great bottle of wine together? We all agreed it would be a perfect opportunity to enhance our friendship. So, let's treat ourselves to a vacation, or rather, an adventure! I propose we drive to London. We leave in two days and stop at all the best wineries we can find along the way, from here to the Channel Tunnel. It will be a trip among friends who share a dream, and all go for it together the old-fashioned way. And if we don't get the bottle in the end, we'll still enjoy a thousand miles on the road laughing, singing, and stopping at vineyards to taste local wines. We could even go through Burgundy. I'll make the itinerary!

Can you imagine? How long has it been since you've done something like that?"

"I've honestly never done such a thing," Roberta replied instinctively with a dreamy look.

Tommaso squeezed Julie's arm and kissed her on the forehead.

"It's a beautiful idea! Difficult to accomplish, but great. Thank you for the support, my friend. I would never have dared to ask so much of you. I could already picture myself flying across the skies alone toward the much-desired bottle."

"Together, it would be a completely different experience!" Interjected Roberta enthusiastically. "Julie is right: it's all or nothing."

"Come on..." the latter shrugged her shoulders. "We can pull it off, I tell you. I have vacation days, and all of you are freelancers, so you can manage your own schedules. You will have time to consult e-mails and communicate with your clients in the evenings, but in the daytime, you will experience the best trip of your life! Of our lives!"

Upon hearing the girl's words, even Luciano, who had remained silent until that moment with a skeptical expression painted on his face, began to smile. Perhaps, between his troubles with the divorce, his new partner, his daughter's tantrums, and the monthly business goals at work, a break and a journey all about wine, friends, and adventure was just what he needed.

"So I understand we are going to London," he said after considering the situation. "Come on, let's order more wine. We need to have a toast!"

CHAPTER 11

"Therefore we maintain that not by laughing but by drinking does man distinguish himself. I don't say drinking simply and absolutely in the strictest sense, for beasts drink as well as man, but I mean drinking cool delicious wine. Take note, friends, that from wine we incline to the divine."
François Rabelais

He had never been much of a man of action, like those who exist in the pages of certain novels or perform amazing stunts on the silver screen. He was a man of quiet manners and peaceful disposition, so the very idea of resorting to violence to accomplish his goals seemed detestable to him.

Yet, here he was: in a car parked on one side of a dark street, slinging a large rifle with a wooden handle and a blackened barrel that gave off bluish highlights. Beside him, Roberta sat in the driver's seat. On her face was a playing card, an ace of clubs. She was also holding a weapon, a silver Old West-style revolver.

Of course, she was always an original woman.

Behind him, motionless and quiet, Julie and Luciano looked out the window. An ace of diamonds hid the girl's face, while the man's mask was an ace of spades. He touched his face and felt the stiff, smooth surface of his card.

I have the ace of hearts. I'm not surprised.

The street was deserted late at night. Looking outside the car window, a few steps from them, a low, square building with large windows and a luxury-hotel-style revolving door also looked deserted. However, it was an illusion. They were well aware that, in reality, the bank was open and operational.

The four friends got out of the car. The rifle felt way heavier in his hands than he expected. He wondered if, when the time came, he would have been able to lift it. The others seemed to have no problem with their respective weapons.

Luciano comfortably handled his voluminous machine gun with a belt loader while Julie held a shiny tray containing several knives placed among Martini cups and large tumblers. They crossed the street and began to walk up the stairs leading to the entrance.

Hopefully, we didn't park the car in a no-parking zone, he thought, hoping that at that time of night, the cops would be sleeping.

The large glass door did not budge. Maybe they got there too early. He felt a sense of frustration mixed with relief. They tried. It was not their fault that the bank was closed.

A moment later, a guy wearing a long red jacket with Austrian knots opened the door from the inside. He reminded him of a circus director he had seen as a child.

Roberta pushed him aside, and they all entered the building. Once in the lobby, Roberta and Luciano began firing shots at the ceiling. The man in the red jacket looked at them displeased, and Tommaso felt ashamed for all the commotion his friends were causing. Even the few customers present at that hour seemed more annoyed than concerned. An elderly lady shook her head as she muttered something to herself. A middle-aged couple diligently kept their spot in the checkout line, waiting their turn.

Perhaps I should also take a number, he thought as he looked around for the self-service machine.

At that point, he saw his three friends huddled behind a counter, arguing animatedly with a well-dressed young man who was probably a cashier. He tried to reach them, but he noticed that the man in the red jacket who had opened the door for them was trying to snatch his rifle. The weapon fell on the floor. His opponent threw himself to the ground, picked it up, and immediately stood back up, pointing the rifle at him. He stepped forward, grabbed the barrel, directed it toward the man's chest, and pulled the trigger. It was a silent shot. The man in the red jacket, with an astonished look on his face, took a few steps back. At that point, fearing the man might fall, Tommaso hurried to get him a chair. The man sat down, pressing his hands on his wounds.

"Can I help you?" he asked him, worried.

"No, thank you. All I can do is pray now."

Unable to bear the scene, he decided that he had to get rid of that cumbersome presence as soon as possible. He picked up the rifle that, in the meantime, had fallen back to the ground and pointed it at the suffering man.

"Stop shaking like that!" protested the latter. "What's the point of shooting?" He suddenly pitied the poor man, so he suggested an idea.

"We can pretend," he told him. "If you play dead and promise me you won't bother us, I'll play along and let you live."

The man seemed to appreciate that solution. He smiled, winked at him, crossed his hands over his chest, and stayed still.

He was relieved to have been able to solve that problem so brilliantly. Now, he had to find his friends, although he could not spot them among the customers. He suddenly panicked, fearing they had abandoned him. Then the scene changed, and there he was. He did not know how, but he found himself in the manager's luxurious office. The bald man was sitting at the head of a shiny rectangular desk. His friends were on either side, with the cards on their faces and guns in their hands. The manager did not seem to mind as he patiently and professionally explained something to them. Behind him, a large rack crammed with bottles covered the entire wall. In it, Tommaso recognized some of his favorite wines. He wondered if he could taste them but did not know who to ask, so he sat down next to the others.

The manager was giving a long, convoluted speech that he struggled to follow. The only thing he understood was that he was inviting them to spend the night inside the bank, claiming that after a good night's sleep, it would have been easier to come to an agreement. His friends agreed as if it was the most natural suggestion in the world. Julie even seemed excited. To solidify the deal, the manager asked to wear the girl's card, but when she took it off her face, she turned into Sara.

Although he was surprised, he was happy to see her again. He thought fate was offering him an opportunity.

Meanwhile, Roberta and Luciano had already laid down on the floor and closed their eyes. He waited for her to settle on the floor as well, then lay down by her side with his back to her. He took out his cell phone to text her, but the phone was so heavy, the keys tiny, and the display unreadable.

Frustrated, he feverishly tried to solve the problem, but holding the phone simply became too unbearable.

Exhausted and resigned, he ultimately gave up. When he turned around to face the girl, he found the man in the red jacket who, while keeping his eyes closed, invited him to stay quiet and stop disturbing the others.

The alarm of a car parked in the yard below his apartment jolted Tommaso awake. He wiped the sweat from his forehead. Thank goodness it had only been one of his absurd nightmares. After checking the time on his smartphone display, he went back to sleep.

CHAPTER 12

The morning of the trip, Rome was engulfed with the typical mist that precedes clear days. The buildings, monuments, and maritime pines—everything seemed weightless, waiting for the city's chaos to begin. On one side of the sky, just above the Imperial Fora, a white, almost transparent moon peered toward the sunrise as if to bid it a final farewell before going to rest.

Tommaso took Via Nazionale, speeding over the dewy glistening cobblestones as the bells of a nearby church gave him his second good morning. Roberta had given him his first good morning a couple of hours earlier. Afraid that he might not hear the alarm clock, she had taken the precaution of calling him while it was still dark. Shortly after that, Luciano and Julie also texted him, alerting him that they were already on their way to Termini, where they were supposed to meet.

I can't believe we are really doing this.

With the opening of the law firm and plenty of work overdue, it had been months since he had taken a vacation.

He felt the euphoria that came with an end-of-year school trip. He was going to have fun together with the people he cared about most, and that thrilled him. However, as he crossed Piazza della Repubblica, captivated by the crystal gushes of the Fountain of the Naiads, he could not help but think he was missing a special person.

Sara would have never come with us. If I got to know her at all over this period of time, she would be the last person in the world who would leave on the spur of the moment to pursue a dream. She is down-to-earth, serious, and practical.

He drove into the sun-drenched Piazza dei Cinquecento, then reached Via Marsala, just outside the station, at the designated area for quick stops. Julie was the first to arrive. She was wearing jeans, a light sweater with her hair down, and a gym bag over her shoulders.

"Hi, Tommy! Have you had breakfast yet? How about a cup of coffee?"

"I already had breakfast. Get in the car!"

" I have a thermos of hot coffee with me just in case," said the girl, settling in the back seat after stuffing her duffel bag into the trunk. "Maybe I made a mistake packing just a few things with me. It's going to be freezing cold in France and on the English Channel."

"'Freezing cold? Maybe chilly," Tommaso replied distractedly. He honked loudly to get Luciano's attention while he was about to cross the street.

"Here I am. Punctual as a Swiss train," he greeted them as he got into the car. "How are you guys? Ready for the adventure?"

"If you don't mind, I will take a nap," said Julie. "I got off so late last night. It was a mess at the wine bar. Once I get some sleep and feel rested, I can take over the wheel, Tommy."

"Later on, I can take over too. I love driving," added Luciano as he wore his sunglasses. "We'll each take turns driving. It's a vacation. Let's not forget that. We all need to relax a bit. In the end, my plan to hide this adventure turned out to be hopeless. Do you know what the consequences were? My ex-wife is furious about this trip but partly relieved that I am not going away with my new girlfriend. My daughter is enraged because I am minding my own business instead of taking her to Japan. As for my new girlfriend, she is also furious because of this trip. "We're off to a good start. You didn't tell me you were one of those men who go off alone or with friends *and girlfriends*! Had I known earlier, believe me, I would have thought about this relationship twice!" she told me."

Tommaso and Julie burst out laughing.

"Sorry, but it was too funny," she apologized. "I actually understand the drama."

"What drama? He is actually very happy right now because he is about to get one thousand and eight hundred kilometers from them. Isn't that right, Luciano?"

"Men understand each other. You are exactly right." Luciano admitted as he laid back in his seat.

Roberta arrived with a tray of pastries and sat in the front. Tommaso stowed the small bright green suitcase in the trunk and climbed back into the car.

"Freshly baked croissants and pastries for everyone!"

"Good thinking, Roby. We need to celebrate this event! I brought coffee."

Julie bit into an almond pastry, and Luciano fished a cream puff from the tray.

"You guys go ahead and celebrate. I'll start the car, or we'll find ourselves stuck in traffic in San Lorenzo until tonight. Do not get crumbs on the seats!"

Two hours later, the Tuscan countryside unfolded like an endless green and gold carpet in all directions. The sun was beating down on the rolling hills, and the vineyards gleamed under the clear sky. The cottages scattered among the fields reminded them of old, lonely peasants who, like poets, were intent on observing the world lying at their feet.

Tommaso felt an inexplicable, tickle-like cheerfulness.

Luciano sat next to him. He was busy looking at Google Maps on his cell phone with prescription glasses lowered to the tip of his nose.

"Guys, this is it," he suddenly said. "Pull over for a minute, Tommy. We need to talk."

They stopped at the yard of a company that sold wine and oil and got out to stretch their legs. Julie stretched her arms wide.

"Welcome to the lands of Chianti! Where should we go now? Antinori or Mulini di Segalari?"

"I vote for Mulini di Segalari. It's a small business that has hard-to-find wines," Tommaso argued. "Have your say, though. Castagneto Carducci is in the province of Livorno, and it's more or less an hour and a half away, while Bargino..."

"Bargino is forty minutes away," pointed out Luciano holding his smartphone in front of his face. "It's that way. I know this area well. My father used to take us on vacation to Tuscany in the summer. We go through Monteriggioni and Colle Val d'Elsa to Tavarnelle, and then we get to Bargino."

"I have never been to Antinori," said Roberta. "They say it's..."

"Huge," Tommaso interrupted her. "I was there a few years ago. It's an incredible sight to behold, really. The wine cellar was carved entirely out of a hillside. It's something between a work of contemporary art and the most insane architectural creation possible. The wooden roof resembles a cork in a corkscrew. I don't even know how to describe it. It spans for I don't even know how many thousands of square meters underground."

"Then let's go there! What are we waiting for? Let's go meet the Marquis!" Roberta clapped her hands, showing all her enthusiasm. "It's even closer than Castagneto!"

"Wait, wait. Let's think about this," Julie raised a hand.

"The signature winery is certainly a worthy sight, but just for a minute, imagine visiting a smaller, cozier winery instead. I have read a lot about Mulini di Segalari. It is magnificent. It's a miniature castle built with its own stone tower, walls, and lush green meadows. Plus, as Tommy said, we could drink more refined wines there that are hard to find elsewhere."

"I know some wine shops in Castagneto that sell Sassicaia by the glass. We could try some old vintage wines," said Tommaso.

"I vote for Mulini di Segalari."

"Me too," reaffirmed Julie.

"I still don't know." Luciano appeared conflicted.

"It's not a question of distance. Antinori appeals to me more, and I've never been there, either. When people talk about wineries, they mostly think of the farmhouse, the medieval castle with the tower, and so on. However, nobody imagines cutting-edge establishments like Antinori, that mix of art and..."

"Yes, but turning over a hill to build the family winery there... I don't know, does it seem ethical?" Insinuated Tommaso jokingly, knowing full well that they chose to build the structure inside a hill to minimize the impact on the landscape.

"You talk like that, but you've been there," retorted Roberta promptly.

"*Touché!*" commented Julie with a laugh.

"Okay, okay. We can go wherever you want," said Tommaso, embarrassed.

"I vote for Antinori," said Luciano.

"Then it's two against two," said Julie, tying her hair in a ponytail.
"Should we toss a coin?"

CHAPTER 13

"Give me books, French wine, fruit, fine weather and a little music played out of doors by somebody I do not know.
"

John Keats

Now that they had made a decision, everyone felt lighter. *Things flow. You just have to let them be,* reflected Tommaso. A moment later, the steering wheel vibrated in his hands, and the car veered sharply to the right, skidding over the edge of the road. He hit the brakes, bringing the car to an abrupt halt, accompanied by a loud squeak. With his heart beating wildly, he turned off the engine. Only then did he realize that his fellow travelers were even more frightened than he was.

Speaking at the same time, they began to ask questions.

"What happened?"

"Is everyone okay?"

"Did you hit a pothole?"

"Did you fall asleep at the wheel? "

"Take it easy," Luciano finally said, in a voice he wished had sounded more confident. He got out of the car, bent down to take a look, and then gave his verdict. "Just as I thought. We have a flat tire."

When they heard the news, everyone breathed a sigh of relief. Everyone except Tommaso.

"Why are you making that face?" Roberta asked him. "We'll help you. You don't have to change the tire by yourself!"

"It's not that..." he replied, not really sure how to continue.

"No way," exclaimed Luciano, spreading his arms wide. "Don't tell me you don't have a spare tire!"

Meanwhile, after getting out of the car, Tommaso opened the trunk and nervously rummaged through it.

Roberta, who came up behind him, rejoiced.

"There it is, the spare tire. You've got it. We'll have it set in ten minutes."

After searching the compartment for another ten seconds, Tommaso got up dejectedly.

"The tire is there, but I don't have the jack."

"What?"

"I don't have the jack. I lent it to someone some time ago and forgot to get it back. It only occurred to me after seeing the flat tire."

"In hindsight, the rest of us should have asked you if everything was all right with the car before leaving for the trip. Maybe it would have come back to you!" regretted Luciano.

"I do have a spare corkscrew, though," joked Tommaso, trying to ease the tension as he pulled a corkscrew out of a case in the trunk and lifted it in the air.

"Come on, it's not the end of the world!" intervened Julie. "We'll call roadside assistance or find a car jack somehow. There must be a house around here. If we find a person who owns a car, they can probably lend us a jack, right? We're not in the Sahara Desert."

Instinctively, everyone looked around and realized they were only surrounded by fields, hills, and patches of trees as far as their eyes could see. Nothing else.

"It may be there," Roberta said, "but I don't see it."

Tommaso felt it his responsibility to find a solution but was undecided. Relying on roadside assistance was probably the most reasonable option. However, he did not love the idea of waiting there indefinitely. Not to mention how expensive and embarrassing it would have been for him. The sun was high, the air mild—searching for someone nearby and asking them for help could have turned out to be a pleasant detour. Roberta and Luciano accepted his suggestion with some hesitation while Julie was ready to back him up. Eventually, the decision was made.

"One of us should stay in the car in case someone comes by," Julie reflected. "We will use our phones to stay in touch. Those who feel like walking, get in line," she concluded, pointing at Tommaso.

Luciano and Roberta looked at each other and immediately agreed at a glance.

"You guys go," Luciano said. "We'll stay and check the car. Whoever solves the problem first will call the others."

Tommaso and Julie walked along the side of the road. The area was quiet and deserted. They walked for several minutes without speaking, absorbed in their thoughts and captivated by the beauty of the view. Without even noticing, they found themselves at the top of the hill. Turning back, they saw the car, which looked small in the distance, while in front of them was a short valley framed by a dense forest beyond which they could glimpse cultivated fields and rows of vines. However, no houses or human presence in sight. It was not encouraging, yet it was early to give up.

"They'll probably work things out," Julie speculated, nodding toward the car. "They'll get help from someone driving by and change the tire."

"What about us, then?"

"We spare ourselves that hard work," laughed Julie. "We enjoy the walk and the clean air! When they're done, they'll pick us up." She covered her eyes from the sun with one hand, then asked, "What's that?"

Tommaso followed the direction of her gaze.

"It looks like a dirt road."

"Maybe it leads to a house."

"Or maybe it leads to some remote field."

"Let's go see," she encouraged him.

Julie's determination won over Tommaso's doubts, and they resumed walking. After about a hundred meters, they took the dirt road. As they followed the path uphill for about two hundred meters, Tommaso noticed tire tracks of various sizes that made him feel hopeful, although the heat made him regret leaving the car. The phone had not rung, meaning Luciano and Roberta had not had better luck.

Once they reached the edge of the woods, they stopped. Walking under the warm sun was one thing, but he did not want to step into the woods. Tommaso could not help but think about the horror movies he saw as a teenager. They all began the same way: a group of friends got into trouble for leaving the main road and venturing to some remote location. However, since he did not want to look like a wimp in front of Julie, he did not protest.

They kept walking without saying a word. Inside the woods, the sun barely filtered through the tree branches. Suddenly, it became cold, and the air was filled with the heavy smell of moss and wet soil. Tommaso felt out of place. Their clothes were not suitable for that unscheduled trek, and their shoes with smooth soles were slippery on the somewhat steep ground. After climbing over yet another log, Julie suddenly stopped.

"Do you think there are animals around here?" she asked.

"What kind of animals?"

"Wild animals, I mean. Like wolves..."

Tommaso looked around.

"I don't think so," he replied, flaunting a confidence he did not have. "I mean, we're not in the Sila region..."

He was starting to get the chills. The road continued through the trees for a few hundred meters more, and there were still no signs of living souls. Suddenly, they heard the sound of an engine and froze. After a few seconds, a pickup truck appeared in the distance, jolting up the dirt road. They could see a man's wrinkled face through the dusty windshield, wearing a baseball cap pulled down to just above his eyebrows.

Although it might have been the rescue they had hoped for, Tommaso hoped the vehicle would not stop. However, with a great squeak of brakes, the vehicle came to a halt right beside them. The man rolled down his window, and Tommaso had the impression that his gaze lingered on Julie's curves.

"Are you guys lost?" the man asked. Deep wrinkles marked his tanned face, but his shoulders looked strong, making it impossible to guess how old he was.

"We got a flat tire," replied Tommaso, "but my jack..."

"Well?"

"My jack broke down," he lied on the spot.

"That's a good one! And how did it break? Those things don't break easily."

"It was old and damaged. Maybe you could lend us yours..."

"And when will I get it back?"

"You could give us a ride down the road," Julie intervened. "It's not even two kilometers. If you take us to our car and lend us your jack, we can change the tire and give it right back to you. It won't take more than ten minutes!"

The man stared at her without changing his expression. He looked calm, but he had not smiled once.

"I need to take this stuff up the road to some friends," the man finally said, pointing to the cargo bed with his thumb. "Come with me. I'll unload the goods, and then I'll give you a ride."

Tommaso and Julie exchanged a glance and read each other's minds.

"It's already late," objected Tommaso. "We were just on our way back."

"Look, if you come with me, you'll still save time. The house is just beyond the woods. I'll unload the drinks and take you back to your car."

"No, thanks. We don't want to bother you," Tommaso tried to deflect. He grabbed his friend by the elbow and started down the road when the man opened the door and got out of his truck.

"What are you afraid of? Come on, get on the back here. It will be a matter of a few minutes. Then I'll take you back down and change your tire."

Julie contemplated the offer.

"We can call Luciano and Roberta from the truck," she whispered to her friend, turning toward him.

They took their places on the truck's bed between crates of soft drinks and gardening tools. The man got back into the driver's seat and started the engine.

"We're two against one, and I did judo as a kid," said Julie, trying to downplay the situation after noticing the concern on her friend's face.

"We're safe then! As long as he doesn't take us to his accomplices."

"Are you serious?"

"No. Yes. I don't know. I'm an office guy. Maybe we should call Luciano."

Julie dialed the number, then gasped.

"No service!"

They looked over the sides of the vehicle, considering whether they should try to get out, just as the truck left the woods and climbed the hill and back into the sunlight. The man kept driving along the dirt road, which soon became flat, crossing plowed fields and vegetable gardens. Tommaso felt responsible for what was happening, while Julie seemed more intrigued than concerned.

Another hundred meters up the road, they could see two rows of poplars and a gate. A dog ran toward them, barking and prancing, following them as they approached a farmhouse with whitewashed walls. Still, aside from the dog, there was not a soul in sight. Only when the truck slowed down did Tommaso hear some shouts coming from the back of the building. It sounded like female voices.

This is it. This jerk has accomplices. They will rape Julie and kill me. Or they will rape me and kill her—or both.

He looked around the truck bed to see if he could spot anything he could use as a weapon. He grabbed a bottle of beer, which seemed like the only viable option, and held it by the neck. The truck parked in the shade of a carport. The man got out and was greeted happily by the dog. As he lowered the sides to allow the two friends to get out, he nodded to the bottle Tommaso was wielding in his hand.

"Do you plan to hit me over the head with that?" he teased. "At least wait until I deliver the drinks first."

Tommaso blushed, put the bottle away, and got down from the back of the truck. The shouts coming from behind the house became more distinct, and it was now clear that people were laughing, celebrating, and singing songs at the top of their lungs.

Julie offered to help carry a crate of soft drinks. Tommaso, still a bit hesitant, did the same. The dog stayed by their side, prancing around them as they walked around the house and reached a courtyard. A long table was set in the center of the yard, and many people were sitting at it. A few girls were singing, others were laughing, and a couple of people looked sleepy. As soon as the diners saw them coming, they greeted them with a long round of applause. A girl wearing a wedding dress left the table and walked toward them.

Tommaso felt relieved. It was like a boulder rolled off his chest. Following Julie's example, he congratulated the bride. When everyone got their drinks, they started singing again. Tommaso felt a little dizzy after the long walk in the sun and that mix of intense emotions that had accompanied him for the last hour, so he was happy when they invited him to sit down with them and have a drink.

Someone brought several bottles of Controguerra white wine from a small producer in Abruzzo to the table. As he wondered why they were drinking wine from another region at a wedding in Tuscany, he realized that he had finished an entire bottle by himself. Meanwhile, a couple of girls, who also did not hold back when filling their glasses, put some flowers in his hair. A group of young men—definitely tipsy—began dancing and dragged the groom to one side of the courtyard. He met Julie's gaze, who had joined the singing group. She raised a hand, holding her cell phone aloft, and Tommaso winked in agreement.

All right. While Julie calls the others, I will close my eyes for just a moment.

Satisfied for having done his duty, he dozed off.

When he woke up, everything around him was silent. All the singing, chanting, and dancing had quieted down. Everyone had either left or disappeared. There was no sign of Julie either. The only being still present was the dog who, comfortably curled up at his feet, stared up at him. Dazed by that unplanned nap and soft-legged, he cursed himself for drinking too much. Suddenly, Julie came out of a side door and walked toward him with a smile on her face.

"Welcome back! I bought a couple of bottles, and another two were a gift. I really like that wine, and judging from how much you drank, I guess you don't mind it either."

Tommaso, still sleepy, looked at his watch.

"We've been gone for hours," he said, concerned. "Luciano and Roberta must be worried sick."

"It's all right, I warned them. Now Giovanni, the gentleman who gave us the ride, will take us back down and change our tire."

Ten minutes later, he felt genuine relief seeing his car on the horizon again. Giovanni changed the tire so fast that he almost matched the speed of a Formula 1 pit stop. Tommaso offered to pay him for his trouble, but the man resolutely refused. He raised his hand to his cap in an awkward military salute and climbed back into his vehicle.

"What the hell happened to you?" asked Roberta, scanning Tommaso's still-sleepy face. "Where did you find that guy?"

There was a note of blame and reproach in his friend's voice. She and Luciano were already annoyed by the car jack's accident, so they had not appreciated the prolonged absence of their two traveling companions. Telling them in detail what happened over the past few hours would certainly not have improved the situation, so Tommaso shrugged his shoulders and, after a nod of agreement with Julie, replied evasively.

"He's a guy from around here. We were walking along a narrow road and had given up hope when he came across us. Now, if you don't mind, I'd like to get some rest."

"He had to be Dionysus in person, given the way you look," Roberta joked, deciding not to let what happened spoil the beginning of what was shaping up to be an adventure they would be unlikely to forget.

Luciano and Julie looked at Tommaso and burst out laughing. Only then did he realize that he still had flowers in his hair. Amidst his friends' comments and jokes, still sluggish from the unexpected hangover, he promptly fell asleep.

CHAPTER 14

"In the countryside, after a hard day's work, men used to raise their wine glass to face level, observe it, and let it catch some light before drinking it with care. Centennial trees followed their fate, century after century, and such slowness approached eternity."
Pierre Sansot

"Bargino is a district of the City of San Casciano, in Val di Pesa. A small urban area located at the foot of Bibbione Castle on one side and Pergolato Castle on the other. On the way to... Hey, are you guys listening to me?"

Roberta lifted her eyes from her smartphone and closed Wikipedia. Luciano was texting while Tommaso seemed busy picking up all the trash he could find in the car.

"Guys, I'll join Julie at the bar to buy a bottle of water," announced the latter. "Sorry, Roby. Of course, I was listening."

"I'll wait in the car. I'll take the opportunity to call home," said Luciano.

Roberta decided to accompany her friend to the bar called The Clock Tower and stepped out of the car.

"Maybe, on the way back, we could drive through Livorno and stop at the Mulini. What do you say?"

"We'll probably be out of money and dead tired, eager to get back to Rome to get some sleep!"

"You're probably right."

Julie was already inside. She had just freshened up in the restroom and ordered a coffee. The three sat down together.

"Do you think we'll be able to visit the winery even though we didn't make reservations?" Asked Roberta. Her eyes sparkled with excitement. "Maybe we'll join a group of

American tourists! It's been ages since I had a different vacation. My husband and I have been going to the same place in Sabaudia for 20 years. I always see the same faces. Don't get me wrong, it's a beautiful place, and the sea is clean, but I really needed to take some time off and get away from my usual life. You are young and..."

"Here she goes! Let's run, Julie. If she keeps this up, by the end of the day, she will ask us to call her grandma," protested Tommaso.

"Roberta, why are you talking like that? You're not old!"

"Julie, I'm fifty. If I'm not old, what am I?"

"A beautiful young woman in her fifties, getting caught up in the traveler's nostalgia."

"I just think I should have done something like this before—maybe with him."

"It doesn't matter when you do it, as long as you do. When you get back, charm him with your stories about this adventure. I'm sure you'll make him want to take a different vacation with you."

"He's depressed, Julie. He hardly gets up from his chair. Ever since he retired, he doesn't talk. He doesn't laugh..." Roberta fell silent, and Julie reflected on how difficult it must be for her friend, who was so bubbly and alive, to have a man beside her who no longer had much desire to have fun.

They left the bar and got back into the car. Luciano was playing a jazz compilation he had put together for the trip and was keeping the beat by beating his palms on his knees.

"All right, but later, we'll listen to The Clash, okay?" suggested Julie.

"And maybe some good ol' songs from the 60s for Auntie," Roberta added, making everyone laugh.

Ten minutes later, Tommaso stopped the car in the Antinori parking lot, not far from a building with a huge wooden roof and a spiral staircase. A young man approached them and welcomed them.

"Do you have a reservation?"

"Of course. 'Four crazy friends on the road,'" replied Luciano. He then turned to his friends, amused. "While waiting for you in the car, I got bored and decided to surprise you, so I made a reservation. Come on, let's go inside. I'm really hungry."

"Four crazy friends on the road?" repeated Roberta, astonished. "You're kidding..."

After quickly checking the list on his tablet, the receptionist confirmed their reservation.

"Four crazy friends on the road, here you are. Follow me. I'll take you to your table. After lunch, you can visit the winery."

The group followed the boy, admiring the spectacular stained glass window that walled the entire restaurant, partially covered by light burgundy-colored curtains. The room used for the restaurant section of the Antinori winery was simply stunning. They ordered a board of Cinta Senese cold cuts and Tuscan bruschetta with black cabbage for appetizers. Then, Tuscan bread soup, shrimp and artichoke salad, Tuscan ox sirloin, and a platter of mixed cheeses. They paired all that food with a 2007 Chianti Classico Riserva Antinori. They savored the wine and enjoyed it while engaging in open conversation during the entire meal.

"Guys, I gotta say, what's the point of working all your life? Think about work for a minute. I've been in the insurance business for almost 30 years. I make a great living, but what kind of life do I have?"

"You don't seem to be doing so badly. I don't understand where you're going with this," Roberta intervened. She looked around for support, finding agreement in the eyes of her friends.

"Maybe you should elaborate," Julie encouraged him.

"Society is the problem, my friends. A while back, I read an article on *The Dissident Intellectual,* a blog I follow. I saved it on my phone. Wait, I have it here. I think it's an excellent representation of the time we're living in. Let me read you an extract from it."

"*The Dissident Intellectual?*" Julie goggled. "Who would that be?"

"A person who thinks and speaks his mind," Luciano cut short. He was intent on scrolling through the files on his smartphone. "Found it. Listen, and tell me if you agree with him. "Western society tries to destroy the will of individuals by preventing them from thinking, reflecting, and improving. That is the reason behind making them work for eight hours every day." Listen to this, 'Everyone's daily life is divided into twenty-four hours. We work for eight hours, so that leaves another sixteen. Out of those sixteen, we sleep for approximately eight hours. That leaves eight hours. On average, people spend at least one hour commuting to the workplace. Now there are seven hours left. Take away another hour for necessary energy storage. I wouldn't call that lunch and dinner, since one hour is not enough to have a proper meal. Let's consider one more for necessary personal hygiene. We have five hours left. One hour is the bare minimum for reading up on the news and surviving in our communication-based society—although we should define it as a "society based on the storage and exponential multiplication of data and information." We still have four hours. Everyone, even people who are single, devote at least one hour a day to family and other social relationships—even if it is a simple phone call or e-mail to parents, acquaintances, or the call center of their phone operator. Finally, we get to the three hours of freedom that our society, on average, allows us on a daily basis.' So, what do you think? Isn't he absolutely right?"

"Time-out, Luciano!" interrupted Tommaso, taking advantage of his friend's pause. "We are having a delicious meal in the restaurant of Marchese Antinori's winery, just a stone's throw from Florence, remember? No sadness allowed! We are on our way to London to bid on and win the bottle of our dreams at an auction. There is no room for bitterness at this table. We were breathing positive energy. Why would we ruin it with paranoia about the time society steals from us?"

"I agree with Tommy," Roberta added while raising her glass.

"Luciano is right, though. They steal our lives," Julie intervened, going in the opposite direction.

"Really? You too?" rebuked Tommaso, giving her a sharp look. In reality, he knew there was a lot of truth in those words shared by his friend, but he wanted to avoid existential distress becoming the theme of the day.

Luciano went on reading, ignoring his friends' various comments.

"He makes a very compelling argument. He continues, 'What can you do in those three hours? Nothing. One cannot do anything significant in three daily hours of freedom that are really just a way of softening one's constraints. Therefore, it is impossible to bring to fruition what, according to our tradition, is the seed of man: "pursuing virtue and knowledge." It is impossible to attain wisdom. Three hours of freedom are not enough to develop our latent faculties, and that is precisely what the system wants, forcing us to stay at the same level. Therefore, it is clear that the whole system in which we live is a complex machine designed to prevent people from developing their latent faculties.'"

"That's enough!" Tommaso intervened again, snatching the smartphone from Luciano's hands and clicking the red button until he heard the beep of the device switching off. "The concept is more than clear. *The Dissident Intellectual* has given us his views on life and time. However, right now, we are enjoying life and wresting our time back from the rules and restrictions in place to keep us slaves, right?"

Julie clapped her hands, and the other two friends nodded.

"The Prince of the Forum is right," Luciano admitted. "Sorry, guys. I got a little carried away. It's the result of years and years of social degradation, smiling and pretending that everything's fine while society ate me from the inside."

Roberta coughed and glared at him.

"Damn, I did it again," Luciano raised his hands in a sign of surrender.

Shortly after that exchange, the friends headed to the cellar to admire the exceptional blend of art and technique that makes Antinori a unique place. In almost sacred silence, they visited the room designated for the maturation of the wine. The years-long process takes place inside barrels arranged in pairs on long rows. They were impressed by the "gravitational" cellar, located deep underground to make the process as natural as possible and allow the ideal temperature to preserve the finished product. Tommaso had visited the place before, but as had happened to him the first time, he was amazed by the sequence of vaults and rooms with glass walls used for tasting that made the entire environment look like a theater.

Their eyes were still full of beauty when, after the visit, they set out on the road to reach the lodging they had selected for the night. It was a b&b just outside Bargino, surrounded by silence. As soon as Tommaso saw it, he thought how nice it would have been to be there with Sara. After a refreshing shower, they met in the lobby for a snack.

"I never imagined I would find actual works of art at Antinori," Roberta suddenly said while flipping through a brochure she took during the visit to the winery entitled 'Antinori Art Project: tastings and other synaesthetic experiences.' "It says here that they host temporary exhibitions by young Italian artists, giving them a lot of exposure. It's a winery and a museum—a museum and a winery. Art and wine. That's true excellence, my friends!"

"Centuries and centuries of history, of love for wine and all things beautiful," agreed Julie.

"However, when Tommaso told the guide that you also manage an art gallery, you turned as red as a tomato!" Luciano mocked her.

"You shut up! You know, with that little speech about free time, you've already burned all the bonuses for today."

"Don't forget the amazing wines we tasted," intervened Julie, trying to move the conversation back on track.

"I'm going to bed," said Tommaso. "I'm exhausted. I even drove drunk today. The bed awaits me. Good night, guys!"

After excusing himself, he went upstairs to the room he shared with Luciano. The bed was tall and old, with a solid wooden frame. The sheets smelled of lavender. Outside the window, the dark countryside stretched under the large, yellow moon that hung halfway across the sky. He opened the windows and took a breath of fresh air. It had been a magnificent day. He picked up his smartphone and opened the chat with Sara. She was offline.

"Good night for now, and good morning for tomorrow when you open your eyes," he typed quickly.

Did I dare too much? Even texting while intoxicated should be a crime.

He fell asleep with a slight smile on his face.

CHAPTER 15

"When wine goes in, strange things come out."
Johann Christoph Friedrich von Schiller

The following morning, Tommaso woke up bright and early. He saw that Luciano's bed was empty. He reached over to the bedside table and grabbed his smartphone.

Sara had seen his message, but she had not replied to it.

What was I thinking? Now she's going to think I'm in love with her and...

He looked out the window and gazed at the landscape in front.

So? What's wrong with that? Isn't that the truth?

He got dressed and went down to the quiet common room. He greeted the boy in charge of serving breakfast and immediately spotted Luciano.

"No, Vicky, I'm not hanging out with my girlfriend. (No, not even with my little girlfriend. – *not sure if to translate this*) No, I—oh, dear God, seriously?"

"Good morning!"

Luciano greeted him back with a nod and continued talking on the phone.

"What do you mean 'do whatever you want?' I told you at least ten times where I'm going and why. I'm with Tommaso. You know him, right? He's the lawyer. Is it too much for a man to take a vacation with his friends? You talk as if I go on trips visiting wineries every week..."

Tommaso walked a few steps away to give his friend some space. Living alone wasn't so bad after all. No one objected to him leaving out of the blue.

However, that realization also held a tinge of bitterness for him.

It is true what they say. People desire what they do not have.

"You are so lucky that you don't have such problems, Tommaso!" Hearing that snapped him out of his musings as if Luciano had just read his mind.

"Did you guys fight all night?"

"Fight...argue. Anyway, no, I got down 45 minutes ago. It is always complicated with Vicky. I can't tell whether she is jealous or just taking a stand."

"Not to put you down, mate, but I reckon it's the second option. Coffee?"

"Coffee? Do you mean a gigantic typical homemade breakfast? In which case, I accept."

They joined Roberta, who was seated at the table, engrossed in reading the newspaper. There was an empty cup and a half-filled glass of juice in front of her.

"Good morning, guys! You're up early."

"I'm here too!" said Julie as she entered the room, stretching as if she had just woken up.

"I'm hungry as hell. Come on, make room for me. How much time do I have to stuff myself?"

"It's six forty. We should leave at seven," replied Tommaso after looking at his watch.

"Great, then we'll even get to have double servings. What's on today's schedule, Mr. Precise?"

Tommaso was about to pull out his notebook from his pocket and stopped just in time. Julie was not going to let him get away with this.

"It's four and a half hours from here to Barolo, five at the most. Should we try to drop in at Accomasso?"

At six minutes past seven in the morning, Tommaso's Golf left the parking lot. This time Julie was driving.

"Would you guys live in a place like that?" asked Luciano after a few minutes, looking at the small towns beyond the window.

"One would certainly enjoy some tranquility there," noted Tommaso.

"Tranquility?" intervened Julie. "That's an understatement. I'd shoot myself out of boredom after two days. What about you, Luciano?"

"Hell no, that was a rhetorical question."

"I, on the other hand, agree with Tommy."

"Thanks, Roby."

"I mean, I agree that it's a quiet place, but it's not for me."

"Come on, Tommy, cheer up!" prodded Julie, elbowing him in the arm.

"When your law firm fails, you can come and retire here.

See, that crumbling little house might be just the thing for you."

"The one with the sheep outside?"

"It's a dog."

"Really?"

"I swear."

"Well, it's one of the most sheep-like dogs I've ever seen."

"It's a Maremma sheepdog, and it's one of the smartest dogs ever," interjected Luciano from behind.

"Of course, if he catches you walking near the flock, you become his snack."

"How cute," whispered Roberta to Luciano while pointing at Tommaso and Julie. "I told Tommy he should ask her out, but he didn't."

"I think he likes someone from a rival firm or something," replied Luciano.

"Yikes, conflict of interest! Now, that problem wouldn't exist with Julie, would it?"

"Well, you know... Young people love drama."

"I can hear you guys," said Tommaso.

Julie, in turn, remained silent. Now that she found out, Roberta specifically asked Tommaso to tell her more about the mysterious lawyer.

"Radio silence," he clammed up.

It was Luciano's turn to be the center of attention then. To make it up to Vicky, who didn't like his sudden departure, his friends suggested he win her back with a bottle of fancy wine.

"Great idea. Does that mean we'll get two bottles of Romanée-Conti 1991? How had I not thought of that before?"

The rest of the drive to Accomasso passed quickly, with Julie refusing to give up the driver's seat. However, When they arrived, she asked to rest for about ten minutes before going into the wine cellar. Roberta stayed back to keep her company while Tommaso and Luciano went ahead.

The winery was located on Route 58 and hidden among the trees at the end of a series of turns connecting La Morra to Annunziata, an area part of the Costigliole d'Asti municipality. The two friends spotted a sign with a rooster drawn on it and the words "Accomasso Lorenzo" written underneath. Luciano opened the door gently. They entered a small room with an old wooden table filled with bottles from all over the world while the shelves displayed wines produced over the years.

"Excuse me, anyone here?" asked Luciano loudly and received no answer.

"Oh, my God! Luciano, look what's on the table! A 2001 Clos de la Roche from Ponsot! Let's grab it and run!" exclaimed Tommaso.

"'How on earth can you even think of such a thing! You're a lawyer, for crying out loud!" retorted Luciano.

A moment later, a door to the side opened, and an elderly, petite man with soft white hair wearing a baseball cap made his entrance.

"When I was young, this part of the basement didn't exist."

"Good morning," Luciano greeted him.

"Since there was no television either, and going out into the countryside at night was dangerous, I used to spend my evenings reading," the man went on without batting an eye. "Dangerous not because there were bad people around, but because there were no streetlights yet. So we had to ride our bicycles with one hand and carry a flashlight with the other, risking falling into the ditch. So at night, I would stay at home and read. An old saying goes, *if speaking is silver, then listening is gold*. Let me tell you, now that I'm old, I finally agree with my elementary school teacher. The Divine Comedy is the best book in the world. It took me just eighty years to figure it out. You can tell that I'm as smart as Gribuja."

"Gribuja?" said Tommaso.

"Yes, *as smart as Gribuja, who hid in a stream in order not to get wet.²*" Where are you folks from?"

"Rome," replied Luciano promptly.

"Oh, you are '*tarùn*' ('rednecks') then! I have a friend from Como who calls me that, so don't take it personally. Anyway, I also enjoy more modern literature, like

---

² Gribuglia is character in Piedmontese folklore.

Camilleri, but I find Eco too convoluted. The sentences are too long. If you write a book, people should enjoy reading it. It's not like you have to show everyone how good you are. As long as you're not Dante Alighieri, that is fine. But those were different times. They had fun back then. Alighieri, Cavalcanti, and all the Florentines had fun with words. For them, it was a game. They challenged each other with poems. Can you imagine? Imagine if, now, the three of us started writing poetry for fun, and in eight hundred years, someone would teach our poems in schools. Such is the power of words."

"Certainly, when you think about it, it's unbelievable. However, I also really like The Divine Comedy. Especially the song of Ulysses," Tommaso interrupted, trying to empathize with the strange host.

"Me too," assured Luciano.

"Anyway," Tommaso resumed the conversation, "congratulations on the winery. It's really cozy! We would love to taste one of your wines. We heard that they are terrific."

"Wine is good when the hostess is beautiful."

"I would agree with that," chuckled Luciano.

"Unfortunately, I don't have any of it left." Said the man dryly.

Tommaso and Luciano looked at each other dumbfounded.

"I don't have any more bottles," reiterated the old man. "All finished. What were you looking for?"

"We were thinking of a 2007 Barolo Riserva Rocche or a 2009 Rocchette."

The old man shook his head grimly.

"I sold them all. I don't have any more bottles!"

"You must have something that we could taste," objected Luciano.

The old man spread his arms and shrugged. However, before he could speak again, two beautiful girls came in smiling through the cellar door.

"Lorenzo!" they greeted him.

"My darlings!"

"How are you?" they asked in unison.

"Now that you're here, wonderful. How about you?"

"All well, thank you. Do you have a bottle of Barolo Rocchette 2008? We'd like to take one to the Red Cross charity auction," the taller one asked in a typical Piedmontese accent.

"Sure! Have a seat. I'll go get it for you," replied the man, walking away from the group and returning shortly after with a bottle of wine.

"Change of plans," whispered Tommaso. "Let's go get ours."

A few minutes later, after looking at Julie's smiling face, Lorenzo Accomasso remembered that he still had a 2007 Rocche Riserva Barolo and a 2009 Rocchette.

As soon as he left the room to get the bottles, Roberta grabbed a bottle from a nearby shelf and placed it in Tommaso's hands.

"Go!" she whispered to him, pointing to the exit.

"What?" her friend protested.

"Didn't you want to steal a bottle? It's your moment," Luciano urged him. He seemed to have changed his mind on the matter.

"I was just saying that, symbolically," Tommaso tried to defend himself by backing away when he heard old Accomasso's footsteps approaching.

Without giving it another moment's thought, Tommaso left the room, followed by Luciano. After leaving the bottle in the car, they went back to the winery as if nothing had happened. Meanwhile, Lorenzo, in addition to the two bottles they requested, had retrieved a 1978 Barolo. When Lorenzo saw Tommaso and Luciano return, he greeted them with a grunt. He filled their glasses only half full, while he was much more generous with the ladies. The wine was garnet in color. The reflections, however, were still vivid and bright orange.

"I hope the wine is to your liking," the winemaker began to speak.

"The year 1978 was not an easy harvest. The summer began with heavy rains, and even when the good weather seemed to be starting, there were frequent thunderstorms. I also had production damage that time, but then, eventually, conditions changed, and for all that was left, it was a great year! I remember that I harvested after mid-October."

"The brightness of this wine is extraordinary," said Tommaso enthusiastically while appreciating the good wine.

"It has a strong and sophisticated smell. Do you also sense the fruity note that goes with cocoa and dried leaves? It also reminds me of wax and a faint dash of makeup powder," said Roberta.

While tasting the wine, they checked for its thickness and substance, and they were all amazed. It was an infinite and concentrated pleasure. When Accomasso walked away again, Tommaso thought it was finally time for Roberta's revenge.

"Well, my friend, you seem to have impressed our winemaker."

"Do you have your notepad with you?" she asked, totally unperturbed.

"Yes, why?"

"You should make use of situations like these to take notes. You might learn something," she concluded with a wink.

"Well, I can certainly learn the art of stealing with dexterity from you," hissed Tommaso.

"Oh, come on. It's just one bottle!"

"One bottle stolen from a poor oblivious winemaker..." remarked Julie, bursting out laughing.

Accomasso reappeared and concluded the tasting by telling them more anecdotes about his youth. After finishing the wine in their glasses, they paid for the two bottles of Barolo, said goodbye to the producer, and returned to the car, feeling a little remorseful for their petty theft.

The next stop on their itinerary was the small town of Barolo. They arrived at the village just before lunchtime. Since they were eagerly waiting for the less-than-frugal dinner they had booked at the *More e Macine* tavern, they opted for a light snack.

"Google points out that there are numerous castles around here that you can visit. There are many choices," said Julie, showing the others her smartphone.

"There is a wide range of castles, but the choice is quite easy," intervened Tommaso, pointing on the map to the central castle of Barolo located in the main square.

"Inside the castle, there is an international museum dedicated to wine and its history. I would say it's an obligatory stop, even if not planned, right?"

The suggestion was unanimously approved, and the visit to the castle turned out to be an unforgettable experience. The same was true for the planned typical dinner, during which they had the opportunity to taste several local wines. Pleased and satisfied with the day spent together, they decided to go to sleep as soon as they left the tavern to be well-rested for the next day.

CHAPTER 16

The following morning, they left the b&b under heavy rain. The sky was a blanket of low clouds the color of molten metal. Thunderous rumbles broke the cold, almost wintery air. The car ride was quiet, except for the notes of Steve Mason's *Oh My Lord* playing from the speakers. Luciano was driving, lost in his thoughts as usual, Julie and Roberta slept in the back seats, and Tommaso was busy studying the map of France they purchased the day before at the gas station. Planning the route on a physical map was a whole different thrill than being guided by the anonymous voice of Google Maps. They crossed the border just before ten o'clock and stopped for refreshments in Chambéry, the Alpine capital of the Savoy department.

"We will reach Beaune in two hundred and sixty-one kilometers," Tommaso calculated once they were seated in a tiny bistro that offered Italian-French cuisine. "Let's continue on Highway A43, which will become A432 and finally A6 just before Beaune. In the meantime, I would order a nice bottle of Mondeuse!" he added after taking a quick glance at the short wine list, happy to try a local wine.

"They also have a 2004 Arbin from Louis Magnin. I would go for that. It's one of the few producers in Savoy I've tried that left me with a good impression," Julie, who was getting sleepy, interjected. "By the way, when we get to

Champagne, would you mind if we dropped by to say hello to my grandparents? I haven't seen them since June. They have several guestrooms, and the family cellar is pretty big. We could spend the night there. What do you say?"

"I would like that," replied Roberta while stroking her hair. "We talked about it even before we left. I don't think there would be any problem as long as we stick to the schedule. As for the wine, let's go for the Magnin!"

"Finally, we can visit our little Julie's winery!" added Luciano. "I can't wait."

They called the waitress and ordered the wine and two local dishes—*tartiflette* and *raclette*. When lunch was over, they resumed their journey heading to Lyon. The car radio was playing *Zombie* by Jamie T. The rain, which took a break while they were in Chambéry, started falling again.

"I can't wait to have dinner at Clos Vougeot tonight and attend the admission ceremony of the Knights!" Roberta said suddenly. "We should thank Luciano for making a reservation at such short notice. It was a miracle."

"I wouldn't call it a miracle. Let's say I had a fair amount of luck! Two days before our crazy plan, I heard from a friend who had seats booked for months. He told me he had to cancel his trip, and I took the chance without hesitating. I thought fate was sending me a sign!"

Everyone inside the Volkswagen Golf shouted with jubilation. Being able to witness such an important ceremony was truly a dream come true for all four of them. They were so excited they felt like teenagers, despite their IDs stating they were respectively 28, 34, 47, and 52 years old. Feeling lighthearted, they passed Lyon and continued toward Mâcon. After about 30 kilometers, Luciano, who had moved to the back seat, fell asleep. Roberta followed within a few minutes. When Julie noticed, she pinched

Tommaso gently, touching the tip of his nose with her index finger.

"You know, Tommy, we've only been on the road for three days, but it feels like I've been traveling around Europe with you guys forever," she quietly admitted to him.

"We're sort of a strange family," he commented without taking his eyes off the map on which he had just circled Morey-Saint-Denis with a fuchsia marker.

"A family—yes, more or less." Julie looked at him from the corner of her eye, then asked him a point-blank question. "So, tell me, do you have a girlfriend?"

"Huh?"

"You heard me."

"No. What about you?"

"I was dating a nice guy. Then, in early summer, out of the blue, he was gone. He vanished. Can you believe that?"

"What if aliens abducted him? Don't be so quick to judge. Maybe right now he's wandering in space in severe pain."

Julie burst out laughing so hard her eyes got teary.

"You're a great girl. You'll find the right one. I'm sure of that."

"Sure. Assuming the right one will find me."

CHAPTER 17

"O my soul, to thy domain gave I all wisdom to drink, all new wines, and also
all immemorially old strong wines of wisdom.
O my soul, every sun shed I upon thee, and every night and every silence and
every longing:——then grewest thou up for me as a vine.
O my soul, exuberant and heavy dost thou now stand forth, a vine with
swelling udders and full clusters of brown golden grapes:——
——Filled and weighted by thy happiness, waiting from superabundance, and yet
ashamed of thy waiting."

Friedrich Nietzsche

They reached Beaune in the afternoon. After wandering for half an hour through Gothic-style mansions and small squares that reminded them of old Art Deco postcards, they arrived at the hotel to leave their bags. Roberta and Luciano immediately went out sightseeing. They planned on buying a few elegant accessories for the evening. However, the Athenaeum library inevitably caught their attention and lured them in. It had wonderful books about wine, many bottles from small producers, and hundreds of items dedicated to lovers of Dionysus's nectar. Meanwhile, Julie had something to eat and fell asleep.

Tommaso took a shower. Half an hour later, comfortably sinking into an armchair, he admired the view through the windows in his room. The half-timbered houses made Beaune look like a town from some Nordic fairy tale. He took a picture of the chimney-filled rooftops and sent it to Sara.

"Look how beautiful this place is!" he wrote.

She replied within a few seconds.

"Wow! It looks like something out of a dream! Where are you? Judging from the rooftops, I'd say you are way up north."

"North, yes. But not that far north. I'm in Burgundy."

That time, she took longer to respond, as if she was thinking carefully about which words to pick.

Or perhaps she simply doesn't care about the topic.

Tommaso was about to put the smartphone away when a notification appeared on his phone. It was a voice message. He felt his heart gallop inside his chest.

Maybe she wants me to hear her voice as she dismisses me to make sure the message is clear.

He pressed play and pulled the phone up to his ear.

"Hi, Tommy. So nice to hear from you!" Her voice was beautiful and sweet. "Everything here is business as usual. Associates are annoying, and the city is noisy and chaotic. I just got home, and all I want is to relax. I think I'll read the new Stephen King novel I bought yesterday."

Oh, you're telling me so many things, Sara.

"I am very happy that you are traveling the world. At least one of us is having a good time these days. I must admit that when I saw the picture you sent me, I suddenly felt a kind of twinge of nostalgia. It's strange because I've never been to Burgundy! Thank you for the thrill. That's it. I should leave alone now. Sorry for going on and on. It's a professional habit! Really, I'll go now. See you soon. You'll be back at some point, right?"

Tommaso replayed the message a dozen times, smiling in disbelief. She had not dismissed it. In fact, quite the contrary.

Her message ended with a question, so I am authorized to answer it.

On a wave of excitement, he started to type something, then froze.

When you think about it, it's not really a question. Of course, I will be back! But then, why ask me? Maybe she does want me to reply. Or maybe, it was just a way to end the conversation, and if I reply, I'll look like a stalker.

He threw the smartphone on the bed and lost himself in the view of the beautiful city. He thought it would have looked even better if Sara were with him. The phone rang, but this time, Luciano's name appeared on the screen. His friend's voice was high-pitched. He was a little out of breath but clearly enthusiastic.

"Are you awake? Am I disturbing you?"

"Of course, I'm awake. And no, you're not disturbing me. I was just relaxing a bit."

"You know, something occurred to me. We are very close to Bruno Clavelier's winery. Since I'm an impulsive guy, I called them and booked a tasting. Of course, given the short notice, I couldn't get a table just for us (*Fabio's comment: "get a table just for us"?? It's not a restaurant!*). They will put us together with a group of Americans who are already waiting. Surely it would have been better to keep it within our group, but that's all I could manage to get. It could be worse, right?"

Listening to his friend, Tommaso began fantasizing about the wines they would soon taste. Bruno Clavelier was unanimously considered one of Burgundy's most interesting biodynamic winemakers. He remembered trying several of his wines, and one, in particular, had made a strong impression—the Premier Cru Chambolle Musigny, la Combe d'Orveaux.

"I absolutely agree," he replied. "How come we didn't have it in our program?"

"We missed it, but now we've made up for it. Snap right up and be in the lobby in five minutes! Oh, I forgot to say that Clavelier only had two seats available. Before confirming them, I called the girls, but they said they were already planning to do some shopping. So we don't have to feel guilty for going without them."

"How far is it?"

"It's barely half an hour's drive. You'll see, we'll have a good time. It's a unique opportunity. Besides, every now and then, it's good to spend some time without girls."

Tommaso sensed a hint of urgency in his friend's voice. He wasn't sure why, but he had the impression that Luciano needed someone to talk to.

"All right. I'll get dressed and join you."

Ten minutes later, Luciano was driving in silence, focused on following the route on the GPS. He seemed to have completely lost the excitement he had earlier during their brief conversation on the phone. Tommaso felt he had to say something to sweep away the unexpected tension that had spread through the air.

"So... tell me about this all-men hangout you seemed so excited about earlier. Why don't you refresh my memory about Clavelier's wines?"

"What?" replied his friend distractedly. He had his gaze fixed on the trees that boarded the country road outside the car window.

"But you are such an *allumeuse*[3]! First, you tease me, and then you ignore me?" Tommaso burst out laughing.

Luciano smiled, but he seemed gloomy.

---

[3] A tease in French.

"You're right. I'm sorry. I didn't even thank you for accepting my invitation, although you might have preferred to get some rest. Please know that I appreciate it very much. I needed to clear my head and have a chat with you alone, that's all. Man to man."

He winced and placed a hand on Tommaso's shoulder.

"Don't get me wrong, I'm really enjoying the trip, and I swear I can't wait for London, the auction, fulfilling our dream, and all that. I mean, this is probably the best thing I've done in years." He paused to think, evidently contemplating what he had just said. "Yes, years. That's the whole point."

"What's going on, my friend?"

"You see, after getting detached from the daily grind, I've started to see my life from a different angle."

"I think I understand what you're saying. We have to get off the merry-go-round to look at it," Tommaso confirmed.

"Exactly. As long as you're on it, you go around in circles, and that's your whole universe. And it works. I mean, generally speaking. It's not perfect, of course, but somehow that life seems to work."

"Are we going to visit a winery, or are you taking me to a philosophy conference?" Tommaso joked to lighten the mood.

"I'm uttering platitudes, I know. Am I boring you?"

"Not at all. I was just joking. And by the way, don't think you're the only one who had these thoughts. To some extent, I have similar feelings. I'm beginning to question everything."

"And you don't feel confused?"

"Well, I'm trying to enjoy everything that's good about the journey while leaving aside the things that are out of my control. But maybe that's just because I'm afraid to face them."

Luciano let out a light nervous laugh, then resumed speaking.

"To tell you the truth, I feel a little tense."

"Tense?"

"Let's just say scared."

Tommaso looked at his friend. He did indeed look worried. His new perspective had perhaps compromised and made him question the certainties his life had revolved around up to that point. Tommaso felt strong empathy for him and felt less alone.

"We still have a few kilometers to go. Tell me everything."

"Are you sure you want to talk about it? Am I annoying you?"

"Since when do friends get annoyed listening to each other's problems?"

"Alright, I'll try to keep it short. Here it is: this trip has forced me to take an unfiltered look at my life and..."

"And?"

"And I like it. I mean, I'm quite satisfied. I think I have accomplished what I wanted—in relation to my possibilities, of course. Since I'm not a Saudi oilman, my goals obviously didn't include sailing around the world on a yacht full of models."

"Would you have liked that?"

"Heck, of course not!"

"Actually, it sounds quite boring. All day lying in the sun drinking ordinary cocktails while the ship's cook makes the same bland meals..."

"That must suck! And what about all those attractive girls buzzing around you while all you want is to be in your office in front of your computer?"

"That's torture, no doubt about it! Also, the stress of docking in a different port every day, not to mention having to throw a party every night on board to avoid appearing antisocial. Unbearable!"

"What a miserable life. I don't think you would have liked it. Personally, I'm glad I don't have to endure it!"

The two friends looked at each other and burst out laughing.

Luciano wiped away his tears and tried to become serious again.

"All kidding aside, I'm quite satisfied. I have accomplished what I wanted to, and I think I did well both professionally and personally with my family. Of course, things don't always go smoothly, but that's part of the game. It's life. It's not a matter of how good or bad you are. It's just how things are sometimes. But now..." He paused and made a vague hand gesture to point at the landscape flowing by outside the car window. "Now that we're on this trip, I 'got off the merry-go-round,' and doubts are creeping up on me."

"What doubts?"

"Doubts about what I'm doing. About everything I've told you so far—about my professional life and... well, my family. I feel more like myself here with you on the road than when I'm absorbed in my daily routine with all its quarrels. Don't get me wrong. I haven't gone crazy. You know me. I can keep my feet on the ground—you know that. But it's as if I have freed myself from some sort of shell. It's as if, traveling with you guys, my energy levels have multiplied, and my senses have been enhanced. Who knows, maybe I'm just feeling like a student going on a field trip at the end of the year. Oh God, what am I talking about? Why is it so hard to elaborate on such a simple concept?"

"Don't worry. I understand what you're saying. It's not that strange, anyway. Since Homer's time, people have been saying that traveling opens the mind."

"Well, Homer aside, I must confess that I am going through a bit of a crisis. Not a big one. Let's say—this big," Luciano resumed, bringing his index and thumb together to mimic a small amount. "It's like looking at myself from the outside and seeing a different man. One who is not me but who I like. A person I'd like to be, let's say. It's like reliving my youth with the awareness of an adult. Some sort of propensity for wonder I thought I had lost forever. The joy of knowing how to feel amazed, you know?"

"You've explained yourself very well."

Although in his calm, quiet, and reasonable way, Luciano was bringing out the fire that burned inside him.

"I wouldn't want to seem pathetic," he continued. "I am aware that it's probably just emotional turmoil due to the new experience. But right now, I get the impression that the real Luciano is the one on the road and that the other guy, the one with a family, a job, and a divorce, the workaholic, the solid, rational, dependable Luciano you all know is just a double playing a role to keep everyone happy and peaceful—as much happy and peaceful as anyone can be in this world, of course."

Tommaso remained silent. Was he going through the same thing? Until that moment, he had devoted all his free time, during which he could let his thoughts run free, to Sara. The voice of the GPS announced their arrival at the destination, relieving him of the need to say something.

He pulled over to the side of the road and entered through the main gate on Route Nationale in Vosne-Romanée. There was a kind of simple and harmonious poetry to the low and essential architecture of the manor house. It was similar to the sober precision of ancient Japanese buildings. The entire wall was covered in wisteria.

"I think I've begun to desire a life like that of a winemaker," Luciano suddenly said, returning to their earlier interrupted conversation. "I could start with something small, you know? Without any ambition, of course. I'd just need a piece of suitable land for a vineyard. It would just be a hobby at first, a way to challenge myself, and I don't mean just as a winemaker. Then, when all the other matters are settled, it might grow into something bigger. Who knows?"

Tommaso merely listened without saying a word. Unable to clearly decipher his own emotions, in a whirlwind of peacefulness, melancholy, and hope, he felt closer to his friend than ever before.

They rang the doorbell, and Clavelier himself came to open it. He had the distinguished sturdy physique of a former rugby player and some graying hair. He wore a blue sweater and a sleeveless jacket with many pockets, suitable for carrying pliers and other vineyard tools. After customary introductions and greetings, he led them inside the winery, informing them that the other American guests would have arrived shortly. While they waited, the two friends admired thousands of bottles stored in iron containers and sorted by type and vintage year. They climbed a small stone staircase that led them to a small tasting room with a large table in the center and bottles of the latest vintage ready for pouring. Clavelier clarified that those wines were intended exclusively for local restaurants and, therefore, were not available to the public. Shortly afterward, the other guests arrived, and the tasting began. Once again, Tommaso was impressed by how elegance and strength blended in the Combe d'Orveaux. When the tasting was over, before they left, they purchased a few cases of wine and asked to have them shipped to Italy.

Just before saying goodbye, Luciano asked Clavelier for a bottle of 1999 Combe d'Orveaux that he'd noticed in the cellar. The winemaker hesitated for a moment but then agreed to sell him the wine for the price of the latest vintage.

"It's not exactly cheap, but it's still a bargain. Besides, uncorking this bottle with Victoria will make her forgive me for this sudden escape with my friends," Luciano said about his purchase as soon as they were out of the cellar.

Tommaso's phone vibrated. It was Julie. She wanted to know what had happened to them.

"We're on our way back," Tommaso replied. "We'll be at the hotel in twenty minutes."

"Is everything okay?"

Tommaso pondered for a few seconds before typing his reply.

"Yes, everything is fine now."

The two friends took one last look at the vineyard, then got back in the car in a very different mood than the one they were in when they arrived.

CHAPTER 18

"Wine is the poetry of Earth."
Mario Soldati

At the scheduled time, they met in the lobby. They had freshened up and got all dressed up for the occasion. The small town of Nuit-Saint-Georges was only a twenty-minute drive from Beaune. The rain had ceased, and an icy wind swept the dark countryside.

The Château du Clos de Vougeot, the castle where the Knights of Wine enthronement ceremony would take place, towered on the horizon.

Since its founding in 1934, the Brotherhood of the Chevaliers du Tastevin has prioritized promoting products from Burgundy, especially wine, and preserving the festivals, traditions, and customs of that land.

When he caught sight of the illuminated chateau, Luciano let out a sudden cry of jubilation, nearly throwing off Roberta, who was driving wrapped in a red Burgundy coat that she bought especially for the occasion. They entered the fortress excited as children. The interior of the château was rough stone. Arches and vaults alternated with areas with large skylights, and tables and chairs were placed everywhere for diners.

"It's amazing, to say the least," commented Julie before checking with the maître d'hôtel, who escorted them to their designated table very close to the stage.

They had just sat down when a voice rose among the general buzz of the room, catching their attention.

"Tommaso! Hey, Tommaso!"

"They're looking for you!" said Luciano, pointing to someone in the crowd. "It's Luca Antonioli! I can't believe it."

"Tommaso looked over and spotted his friend sitting in a wheelchair, looking elegant as ever. Making his way through dozens of guests, he joined him.

"Luca, what a surprise! What are you doing here?"

"The same thing you're doing here! Amazing, isn't it? We live two kilometers away but never see each other, and then we meet in Burgundy! I see you are with your usual friends."

Luca turned in the direction of the group and waved.

"Yes, we are headed to London. We're taking a road trip before the winter."

"We will leave tomorrow for Paris and stay there a few days before returning to Rome. After this event, I will take you to a place nearby where there is dancing all night, so get ready."

At that very moment, the members of the Brotherhood of Enthronement, dressed in long fiery red robes with gold hems, made their entrance accompanied by trumpet blasts. Tommaso rushed to his seat.

"What is Luca doing here?" asked Julie.

"Who is that boy?" asked Roberta.

"Luca and I went to high school together. He is also here with friends.

He suggested we go dancing with him when the ceremony is over."

"Let's see if we'll be able to!" laughed Luciano.

Meanwhile, the men in robes had settled on the stage. One of them began to do the honors, explaining the significance of the appointment of the new Wine Knights. The atmosphere in the venue heated up quickly amidst red faces, the aromas of food, and the constant bustle of poised waiters swiftly hovering between tables with trays filled with delicacies and bottles of wine. The entire menu contained local dishes, and the four friends enjoyed several of them, all cooked with wine. They started with the typical *Pauchouse*, a soup made of freshwater fish cooked in white wine and served with buttered bread, paired with a Bourgogne Chardonnay 2014 Tasteviné.

The more daring palates ordered the famous escargot à la Bourguignonne for the second course, accompanied by a 2011 Beaune 1er Cru Les Bressandes. The more cautious palates opted for *coq au vin*, a dish with chicken cooked in red wine and flavored with herbs and vegetables. The recipe dates back to the time of Julius Caesar, and it was paired with a Clos-Vougeot Grand Cru 2011 Tasteviné. The dinner ended with the classic *Panpepato*, a dessert made of rye flour, honey, oranges, candied lemons, anise, and cinnamon, known for its digestive qualities.

When the banquet was over, the enthronement ceremony began. Luciano and Roberta moved to the foot of the stage to get a better view and take photographs. Amidst the applause, there were toasts from diners and jubilant songs played by the orchestra during the pauses between statements made by the master of ceremonies. Tommaso felt as happy as he had in a long time. The good wine, the feeling of freedom he had experienced in the last few hours, the companionship of friends, the distance from home, the duties of the firm, the prospect of winning the auction in London, and finally uncorking a bottle of Romanée-Conti from 1991 made him happy. Everything seemed to be part of a truly perfect mechanism.

When they left the ceremony, it was late at night. They were pumped up and decided to accept Luca's proposal, who, in the meantime, had already moved to a club not far away. It was halfway between the countryside and the city. The *Aubergine* looked like a violet flying saucer resting among the vineyards. Stroboscopic beams of light crossed the still cloud-covered sky. The air had become even colder and more humid.

"Guys, is it okay if we go inside, have a drink, say hi to Luca, and then all go to bed?" suggested Tommaso, wrapping himself in his jacket. No one had any objections.

"One day, some of us will get on that stage too, I'm sure," suddenly said Luciano, thinking back to the ceremony that had just ended.

"And the others will absolutely have to be in the hall cheering!" exclaimed Julie, raising her eyes from her smartphone.

"By the way, I'm not drinking anymore for tonight. I'm good."

"Julie, what does the club's name mean?" asked Tommy.

"Eggplant," replied the girl. A gust of wind had disheveled her hair across her face.

"You see, this is why I always keep it tied up," she grumbled.

"Eggplant? Really? How can you call a club eggplant?" commented Luciano.

"Well, it has purple walls," noted Tommaso.

"In Barcelona, there is a nightclub called *Cebolla*, meaning Onion. You're not the man of the world you pretend to be, Luciano."

"I'm just plain old!" replied Luciano as he entered the club and immediately entrusted his hat to the two cloakroom attendants dressed in elegant purple suits.

They walked through a long Plexiglas tunnel with iridescent colors and found themselves in a very large room furnished in a white minimal-fantasy style. The dance club was lit by fluorescent neon lights that looked like liquid. The bar counter took up an entire wall, while ottomans, round tables, armchairs, and sofas were scattered around the room. The furniture seemed to replicate the interior of a spaceship. A pleasant hypnotic mix of house, chill-out, and drum&bass music permeated the room.

Luciano appeared out of nowhere carrying a transparent tray with three plastic flutes. The tray had very thin strands of LED strips, like blue veins.

"They offered them to me at the entrance. I think it's an amazing supermarket champagne," he laughed.

Sitting at one of the small tables near the bar, Luca spotted Tommaso and called him loudly, waving.

"He seems to be on a roll," observed Julie, scratching her temple.

"Does your friend like wild partying?"

"Absolutely. He'll try to make us drink like sponges, but we'll resist and bail at the first opportunity."

"Come on, sit with us, guys!" shouted Luca, spreading his arms welcomingly.

He introduced himself, shook hands with Julie and Roberta, and ordered drinks for everyone.

"Tell me, what have you guys been up to today?"

"As I said, we're on a trip visiting wineries," exclaimed Tommaso as he sat beside his friend's wheelchair.

"We're on a tight schedule, so we have to rush most of our visits. We're only stopping at the obvious places, but we're having fun, and that's what counts."

"Where are you headed?"

"To London," replied Luciano. "We'll come back with empty pockets, but we'll be happy!"

A young, tall waiter with a blonde fringe and a boyish smile placed some brightly colored cocktails on the coffee table. Roberta, intent on observing the room, did not hear him coming due to the noise in the background. When she turned around, she involuntarily bumped her shoulder into his elbow. Embarrassed, she stammered a few apologetic words and tried to help him but failed miserably and spilled more cocktails on the floor.

Luca burst out laughing.

"Sometimes, you try to fix something and make things worse."

Roberta felt even more mortified.

The waiter smiled at her and, speaking pretty good Italian, tried to reassure her.

"It's okay, really," he said.

Annoyed by Luca's comment and slightly overwhelmed by the waiter's bright gaze, Roberta was unable to say anything. To chase away that unpleasant feeling, she ignored her friends' chatter and studied the dance club. However, she struggled to focus on any detail. Her mind kept running back to the smile of that handsome waiter who had spoken to her. She chided herself for that thought. She did not want to appear anti-social, so she tried to retune herself to the conversation at the table, but her attempt was futile.

The waiter returned for a second round of cocktails, and Roberta felt excited. Was she hallucinating, or did his smile widen when he addressed her? Again, she got mad at herself for that ridiculous observation.

"He is offering us the house cocktail. If I understand correctly, it has gin, vodka, lime, and some other ingredients. What do you guys think?" Tommaso asked the group.

Everyone was enthusiastic about it.

Realizing that his customers did not understand the exact composition of the cocktail, the waiter repeated the ingredients more slowly, trying to translate them into Italian one by one. Roberta noticed the young man's gaze, and once again, she thought he was paying particular attention to her. She was flattered but did not want to admit it. She preferred to assume the waiter thought she was a bit dumb, so he explained everything like she was an old aunt.

"Yes, yes, I understand!" she answered him hastily, only to regret it soon after.

Fortunately, Luca took care of melting the tension, monopolizing the conversation.

The second cocktail of the evening managed to relax the woman, who finally admitted to herself that she had a crush on the young waiter, despite the age difference.

Although, was he that much younger than she was? How old could that young man be? Maybe thirty-five. After all, he was a grown man. After finishing that quick analysis and absolving herself of her thoughts, Roberta felt much better. However, she still regretted dismissing him so abruptly and vowed to make up for it as soon as he returned for a new order, but when the waiter came back to the table, instead of a natural smile, Roberta had a nonsensical grimace on her face.

She observed him moving around the club and noticed many other beautiful women and younger girls in the room. Yet, he did not smile at them as he had at her. She went to the restroom to retouch her makeup, then walked around the club before returning to her table. Her waiter was talking to the barman with his back facing her. She took the opportunity to examine him quietly. He was even taller than he had seemed to her at first. His blond fringe kept falling over his right eyebrow, and from time to time, he moved it out of the way with an automatic gesture that looked awfully sexy. His shoulders were broad and proportionate, and he moved with a vigorous grace. He was probably a sportsman—but not a gymnast. Perhaps a tennis player or a swimmer. However, he also looked somewhat intellectual, maybe because of the broad forehead or the wry crease in his mouth.

As she played with her imagination, she felt a cold chill run down her spine when the reflection in the bar mirror revealed that the waiter was smiling back at her.

She had been caught, so now she had nothing left to lose. She approached the bar counter with sudden ease.

The boy held out his hand to her and introduced himself.

"Julian."

"Nice to meet you. I'm Roberta."

"Rome is a beautiful city, after all. But it's boring. Here, they know how to have fun!" shouted Luca over the music.

"Did you see how amazing the enthronement ceremony was? It was pure cheerfulness and madness."

"All thanks to the good wine," suggested Julie.

"'You are beautiful! Would I upset anyone if I gave you too many compliments, or are you single?"

"I'm single..."

"Then let's go dancing, come on! I can't get up, but you can twirl me around like a butterfly!"

"I don't know how to dance," objected the embarrassed girl.

"Not to be rude, dude, but we are really tired," Tommaso intervened to her aid.

"I won't take no for an answer," Luca interrupted him, grabbing Julie's hands.

"Why not? Let's dance!" said Luciano as he stood up.

Tommaso remained seated, taking pictures of his friends. Not even the good wine and cocktails he drank that evening could overcome his shyness.

CHAPTER 19

"I am beauty and love, I am friendship, your comfort, I am the one who forgets and forgives: the spirit of wine."
William Ernest Henley

An unreal silence prevailed in the car. Tommaso's eyes were glued to the line of asphalt rolling out into the night. Next to him, Luciano, only seemingly dozing off, gazed at the landscape scrolling by outside the window. It was Julie who interrupted that uneasy situation.

"Guys, we should have at least driven him. He was completely drunk!"

"I don't want to talk about it," said Luciano, lowering the window a little and letting a blast of icy air into the passenger compartment.

"At my age, I can't be around wild kids. I already have a daughter who tests me considerably in that regard. Forgive me, Julie, but what happened is not our responsibility."

"It's not about responsibility," she retorted. "We should have helped him. He doesn't speak a word of French and—."

"And he is in France with his friends," Tommaso concluded, siding with Luciano.

"Taking him to the hospital would have only added more unnecessary chaos. Besides, it's not like anything serious happened. I think he just hit his head! It was funny, though!"

"Tommy! We're talking about a guy who..."

"No, Julie, I know what you mean, and you're dead wrong. I've known him for 20 years. He is one of those guys who likes to have a great time! The fact that he's in a wheelchair doesn't change anything. Besides, we didn't abandon him."

"Those guys with him were all drunk. While the paramedics carried him out on a stretcher, they were laughing like crazy!" protested Julie again, but her words only made Tommaso and Luciano laugh even harder.

The tension melted away. It had been a good evening, after all, and it was in part thanks to Luca's exuberance.

"We'll give him a call tomorrow," added Tommaso.

"There isn't a party where Luca hasn't tipped over, I assure you. Oh, the scenes I've witnessed..."

"Let's hope he didn't break his nose. He was bleeding like a fountain."

"He didn't break anything. He's used to it!"

" I mean, trying to jump a step to get on the runway was not a great idea..."

"That's right, but Luca is Luca. Don't worry. He has a thick skull. Don't let him ruin the memory of this evening."

Julie smiled and patted Tommaso's shoulder.

"Can you imagine?" she said suddenly, changing the subject.

"In a few days, I will finally introduce you to my grandparents. I have been talking about you for two years. Now they will be able to meet you and know who I spend my free evenings with."

"They will be very disappointed, I'm afraid," commented Luciano.

"I suppose they aspired to something better for their only granddaughter!"

"Shut up!"

"Hey, speaking of disappointments and satisfactions..." continued Luciano, nodding toward Roberta, who had not opened her mouth since they got in the car.

"There's someone here who I think didn't have a disappointing night. What happened? At one point, you completely disappeared..."

Roberta blushed, squirming in the back seat.

"I wasn't feeling very well, so I left the club to get some air."

The two men, noticing her embarrassment, saw fit not to reply.

However, Julie, who knew how her friend had spent the night, burst out laughing.

"So that's how you found out the club also provides extra services!"

At that point, they all laughed. When they arrived at the hotel, they parked the car and went to sleep.

CHAPTER 20

"So does wine have a longer life than ours? Well, we fragile human creatures shall wreak our revenge by drinking it all up. In wine resides life"
Petronio Arbitro

Tommaso got to Luciano's house last. He brought a selection of English cheeses, including a Lincolnshire Poacher, as agreed with the others the day before, and foie gras purchased from a renowned delicatessen in his neighborhood. He also had a bottle of Sauternes, Crème de Tête from Château Gilette, which he preferred to the noble Château D'Yquem. He sat at the table and noticed his friends staring at him with strange smiles. "What is it?" he asked.

Julie and Roberta lifted the tablecloth and took something from under the table. Luciano observed the scene, amused. When the two friends placed the bottle on the table, the smiles became shouts of jubilation.

Tommaso himself could not refrain from clapping his hands.

"How did you get it? Where did you find it?"

"Happy birthday, Tommy!"

His friends sang "Happy birthday" flatly and placed the bottle of Romanée-Conti '91 he had longed for right in front of him.

"Don't ask us how we got it," Luciano corrected him, "but how we managed to wait until your birthday to uncork it! To Tommaso!"

So, with trembling hands and a big smile, Tommaso uncorked the bottle.

"The wine glasses, the wine glasses!" he shouted, and his friends extended their glasses.

With taste buds ready to savor that unmentionable delight, Tommaso served everyone, careful not to waste a single drop. When the glasses were filled, it was time to finally taste the wine.

"What the hell!" exclaimed Tommaso with widened eyes.

Roberta looked at Luciano, who turned to Julie.

"It's a Cabernet Franc from the supermarket! Are you serious?" blurted Tommaso, unable to comprehend how they could pull such a stupid prank on him.

"Are you guys kidding me?!"

"Tommaso, wait!" Luciano jolted to his feet.

"No one is joking here, we paid almost nine thousand euros for this bottle, but it is clearly counterfeit wine. I also smell Cabernet Sauvignon in it. What do you think, Roby?"

The woman brought her hands to her face. Julie kept shaking her head.

"You got ripped off!" shouted Tommaso.

"Nine thousand euros for a bottle of mixed grapes!"

"Watch your mouth, boy. This was your birthday present! How is it our fault? Do we look like people with nine thousand euros to throw into supermarket wine just for the thrill of pulling a prank on you?"

After Luciano's words, Roberta stood up and left the room. They heard the front door slam a few moments later.

"You really are ungrateful, Tommy," Julie recoiled, walking away from the room.

At that point, Luciano's ex-wife entered the room.

"Come to the other room. We need to talk. I'm going to file for divorce."

Luciano burst into desperate weeping.

Tommaso jerked awake, his fingers clinging to the sheet. It took him a few moments to realize where he was.

"Another damn nightmare!" he cussed after turning on the bedside lamp. "Damn, that felt so real!"

He got up, drank a glass of water, and looked at his smartphone. He had received a few WhatsApp messages, and one was from Sara.

"How did it go today? Did you drink any good wines?"

He quickly typed in the answer.

"Actually, I just had a nightmare. Maybe I ate too much. How nice to hear from you! Anyway, all good, and you?"

The final question was supposed to make her feel legitimized to answer him. Once he put the phone back on the bedside table, he slipped under the covers and fell back into a deep sleep.

CHAPTER 21

"I could not live without Champagne. In victory I deserve it, in defeat I need it."

Winston Churchill

The following morning, the faces of the four friends bore the signs of the long car ride and wild night. While jokingly complaining and teasing each other, they compared how tired they were.

"We're still in great shape," Luciano judged, intent on buttering a crusty baguette. "We'll come out of this adventure rejuvenated, and as far as I'm concerned, no Japanese trip can put me in a bind."

"Speak for yourself," Roberta protested. "I feel like a wreck. Maybe I should buy a mattress, lock myself in the trunk and get some sleep. You can wake me up when we get to the auction. Or better yet, right after."

Tommaso stretched, sighing. He was having his third cup of coffee.

"The search for the Holy Grail takes effort, my friends, but the satisfaction will be as sweet as honey. In fact, it will be as sweet as a 1991 Romanée-Conti."

They all laughed, except for Julie. The girl removed a brioche crumb from her lips and then turned to Tommaso.

"Did they ever find it?"

"What?"

"The Grail."

Tommaso was caught off guard. He looked at the others for help, but judging from their vacant expressions, he realized he had to get himself out of trouble.

"I can't really remember," he admitted. "I think they did. Now, I couldn't tell you off the top of my head what happened. But even then, it was a matter of finding a goblet. Although it wasn't filled with wine, I'd say it's pretty much the same thing."

Julie quickly consulted Google on her smartphone.

"It says here that the Grail alludes to esoteric or initiatory knowledge, reserved for those who will be able to embrace its mystery, proving themselves worthy to receive the magical power it holds."

"It sure sounds like it's talking about us," joked Tommaso.

"Maybe. But it also says that the quest will test the will and spirit of the participants and that, regardless of the outcome, one will come out of the quest changed."

The room fell silent. Luciano intervened to lighten the mood.

"Hey, we are just four friends going to an auction. I'm pretty sure those looking for the Grail didn't get a chance to buy it—not even in installments!"

After breakfast, they resumed their journey. The sun finally managed to peep through the clouds, revealing the gentle shapes of the landscape. That enchanting mix of neat vineyards, hills dotted with cottages, and the scent of grass and earth suddenly swept away the fatigue of the journey, breaking through the eyes and hearts of the four friends. They made a brief stop at a small delicatessen to buy a few loaves of bread, half a dozen sausages, some cheese, and two bottles of Champagne, which they decided to enjoy in a lay-by a little further on, surrounded by the colors and smells of the countryside. After their break, they would set off again toward Reims, where they had scheduled a visit to the Veuve Clicquot winery. They ate in silence, immersed in that simple yet all-encompassing beauty, each contemplating their own thoughts. After finishing their lunch, Tommaso took a few photos with his smartphone, planning to send them to Sara later. He wanted to keep that small but precious connection with her.

Reims greeted them with vibrant colors, majestic appearance, and lively streets. The top of Notre Dame de Reims, visible above the rooftops, revealed itself to their eyes at every turn as if it were trying to draw them in. However, they postponed their visit to the cathedral until the following day and went straight to the hotel. Before splitting up to go to their separate rooms, Tommaso called a brief meeting—a 'council of war,' as he called it.

"Let's go easy on the tastings today," he exhorted. "Or at least let's remember to check what is included in the visit and what is not. I don't need to remind you that we are in the homeland of Champagne, and our resources are not unlimited. After all, we could use some extra money during the auction."

"I agree. Can I be the group accountant?" applied Roberta. "I'll keep you guys on a tight rein. We will go through the guided tour like ascetics, indifferent to any temptation!"

"Oh my God!" protested Luciano, laughing. "Are we going to visit a winery or a convent?"

"I know you," replied Roberta imperturbably. "And I will keep an eye on all of you!"

"All right," Tommaso wrapped the impromptu assembly. He could not wait to lie in bed and send the photos to Sara. "Roberta has been promoted to group accountant."

He went to his room, unpacked his suitcase without much care, and took a quick shower. Fifteen minutes later, Tommaso began scrolling through his photographs and wondered what Sara was doing. If he sent the pictures, would she receive them and look at them right away, or would she wait for a more convenient time to take her time and enjoy them? Also, most importantly, would she like them, or would she reply to him just out of politeness, perhaps pretending to be enthusiastic about them while not really caring? Tommaso suddenly felt discouraged. Uncertain of what to do, he stalled for several minutes before pressing the send button. After finally summoning the courage to do it, he immediately switched off his phone, placed it back on the nightstand, and fell asleep. He woke up a couple of hours later, changed, and went downstairs to the lobby. His fellow travelers were already there, punctual for their scheduled appointment.

"As the group's newly appointed accountant," Roberta jokingly warned them, "I would like to remind you that from now on, before you take any financial initiative, you must consult me. So I advise you to be nice to me."

"We always are," Luciano retorted, surprising himself at how seriously he made that remark.

"Come on..." said Roberta. Taken aback by Luciano's words, she felt slightly embarrassed by the turn the conversation was taking. "Don't try to bribe me right away."

When they arrived at Maison Veuve Clicquot, they entered a low, clean building with stained glass windows at the end of a long driveway. Roberta, faithful to her new role, took care of paying for the visit. When the guide arrived, they and 20 other visitors started following her with reverent awe.

Although Tommaso had looked at several photos and videos of the winery online, as he walked down the stairs, numbered and lit by amber neon, into the network of tunnels and underground caves illuminated by soft lights, he felt an intense thrill. He let the guide's hypnotic narration lull him as he walked among the shelves containing millions of bottles, and footsteps echoed off rock walls. He could tell his friends felt the same way, seeing his own emotions reflected in their silent expressions.

They took their first break to taste Maison's classic *sans année*. To pair the wine, they served Tome de Montagne, a salty cheese with a creamy texture made from the milk of Savoy mountain cows. When the tour resumed, the visitors scattered. Champagne began to take its toll on some of them, who stayed behind, while others, after sharing the underground route together, felt the need to discuss their impressions and experience with their respective fellow travelers.

For whatever reason, Tommaso found himself surrounded by a small group of Germans. He started looking around for his friends but could not find them. He searched a couple of side alcoves but only found couples seeking some privacy. All of a sudden, someone pulled by the sleeve of his jacket. Julie, holding a glass, pulled him aside.

"I was looking for..."

"Yes, I know. I was looking for them too," Julie interrupted him. "But maybe they don't want to be found."

It took him a couple of seconds to understand what the girl meant. When he understood, he shook his head.

"No way. They were in the front earlier with some American couples. We simply fell behind, but if we hurry, we can catch up with them."

"Later. Will you come with me to get another drink? All this walking down here made me thirsty."

Julie seemed a little tipsy. When they returned to the tasting table, Tommaso realized they were the only ones there. His friend had a few more glasses of wine, and he did the same to keep her company.

"Let's join the others," he finally suggested, feeling vaguely uncomfortable. "They're probably getting worried."

They entered the tunnel again. It was empty now, and their footsteps echoed thunderously in the underground passage. They stopped at a junction, undecided about which way to go.

"This way," he guessed, far from sure.

"I don't think so. Can't you see it's all dark? We have to follow the lights."

"What lights?"

Julie pointed to the lighted alcoves.

"That just looks like a side passage to me. I think it's a dead end."

"Are you afraid of getting lost? We're in a cellar, not the catacombs of Paris. Come on, don't make me beg you."

Persuaded by his friend's determination more than her words,

Tommaso followed Julie down the side tunnel. After just a few steps, the road was blocked by a rock wall.

"Oops, I guess I was wrong!" admitted Julie, grimacing and tilting her head to the side.

"It happens. Let's go back.

"Wait. I'm tired. All those stairs... Let's sit down for a minute."

"Where?"

Julie pointed to the rails behind which the lights were fixed, a few steps away from a wall of bottles aging *sur lattes*.

"Here, just a moment. My head is spinning."

"Maybe we should go outside if you've had too much to drink..."

"It's not that. I can handle alcohol much better than all of you. It's just that down here—the dim lights, the silence—it feels like the air is vibrating."

"It's the hum of the lights."

Julie put a hand on Tommaso's wrist and smiled at him.

"You're so wise," she teased him. "Come on, sit here with me."

He complied. They remained silent for a few seconds, listening to the muffled voices and footsteps coming from the other corridors.

"We shouldn't be here," said Tommaso. "We should be with the group."

"Is it forbidden to sit down?"

"I don't know. Maybe the guide is getting worried."

"So what if she is? You know, I was thinking about what Luciano said the other day. Maybe he's right. I'm not saying completely, just partially. If we don't take our share of freedom ourselves, no one will give it to us."

Sitting by her side, shoulder to shoulder, Tommaso did not know where Julie was going with this. The girl resumed her speech. She sounded serious.

"Everyday life is like a theater backdrop, and people risk becoming characters in a play. Their characters resemble their real personalities, and they are repetitive and predictable. Because they do and say the same things over and over, no one pays attention to those characters anymore. But if we moved them out of that background, they would go back to being people capable of being surprising, and others would notice them. That's what's happening to me on this trip, with you guys." She paused for a moment. "Do you think I'm talking nonsense?"

"No, on the contrary. Now that you point it out, I realize that maybe the same thing is happening to me. Life forces us to play a part, but things are different now. Now we are who we are."

Julie sighed.

"I'm glad you understand me. I care about what you think of me. I'm not as confident as I'd like to seem."

"I think it's simply because we are all vulnerable," Tommaso reflected. "To cope with life, just like some animals do who puff up and raise their fur to look bigger, we pretend to be tougher than we really are."

"I like that analogy," observed Julie. "We do it to defend ourselves from predators, which in our case are those who might take advantage of our feelings. We wear a suit of armor. Too bad it's paper armor, or rather it becomes that on certain occasions."

"I think it's natural to protect our feelings."

"Protect them, but don't hide them."

They heard footsteps. An attendant passed by in the main tunnel, pushing a cart full of empty bottles and glasses. He did not notice their presence.

"I don't think we hide them," resumed Tommaso, almost speaking to himself. "But neither do we disclose them so easily. They are the most intimate things we have, which we only share with people..."

"That we trust," Julie finished his sentence. "If things are as you say, apparently, you don't trust us. Or, at least, you don't trust me."

"Why do you say that?"

Julie crossed her legs. In doing so, she slipped to the side and leaned on Tommaso to avoid falling. Even after regaining her balance, she did not let go.

"You've been different for the past few days. It's obvious."

"It's because of what we said earlier. When we get out of our daily routine, we're all a little different."

"It's not that. You were different even before we left."

Tommaso tried to ignore the pleasant feeling of Julie's hand on his arm.

"I don't understand..."

"Never mind. Let's just leave it at that."

"Why? We are friends, aren't we? You said so. And no one else is here. It stays between you and me."

"It's just that..." Julie swallowed. "You used to look at me differently. For the past few days, however, it's been like you don't even see me. I didn't notice before, but it's pretty obvious now that you're paying less attention to me."

She slid her hand down Tommaso's arm, resting it on the back of his hand.

"Some say you only realize how important something is when you're about to lose it, and it's true," she whispered, getting even closer to him. "That girl, Sara. Ever since you met her, you've been different."

Sara! At that moment, Tommaso realized he had forgotten to switch on his phone, and he wished she was sitting next to him instead of his friend. He stood up, gently squeezing Julie's wrist and pulling her along.

"I think I should put this away," Julie said, pointing to the empty glass she was still holding tightly in one hand.

Tommaso searched for the right words to tell her that although his heart beat for another woman, he felt immense affection for her. He could not find them, but fortunately, he did not need to. Julie did not look sad but relieved, as if a weight had been lifted off her shoulders. "At least we talked things out and were sincere with each other. I feel like now we're even closer," she clarified as if she had read his mind.

They hugged and held each other's bodies close for a few seconds. Then, they rejoined the group in the main gallery, which had reassembled in another cave, waiting to return to the surface. When Luciano and Roberta saw them, they smiled mischievously.

"There you are," exclaimed the woman. "Where have you been hiding?"

"We got lost," tried to divert Tommaso.

"But now we're all together again," concluded Julie before her friends could add anything else.

By the time they exited the cellar, it was dark. On the way back, Tommaso kept his phone off a little longer. Partly out of discretion toward Julie but also to prolong that pleasant wait. They ate at a diner in Place Drouet-d'Erlon, surrounded by a cosmopolitan crowd. Inspired by the weather, they ordered paprika-marinated duck breast—served with sweet and sour sauce and orange compote—and beef sirloin with bell pepper sauce. They paired the meal with a bottle of Pinot Noir with intense fruity hints of cherry, blackberry, and currant. They concluded dinner by sharing a lemon meringue, feeling satisfied with the food and wine. Before leaving the diner, they quickly reviewed the next day's schedule, which included finally meeting Julie's grandparents.

CHAPTER 22

"When I die, bury me in a vineyard, so that I can give back to the
earth all that I have drunk in my life."
Francesco Guccini

Julie's grandparents lived on a refurbished farm that
looked more like a *buen ritiro* than a place of business.
Tommaso believed that, with the proper modifications, it
could become a fancy b&b with flair.

All three friends barely spoke French, but with Julie's
help, they managed to communicate. Despite his age,
Bertrand, Julie's grandfather, looked handsome and
vigorous and demonstrated from the beginning that he
could speak a universal language. He did so by having his
guests sit on the veranda and opening a few bottles from
his wine production.

They started with a bottle of still-white wine. Tommaso
appreciated the flavors of white peach, citrus, and almond,
as well as some notes of lemon cream that gradually
emerged in the wine. It was very fresh on the palate and
had a slightly buttery texture. Next, they moved on to a
creamy, velvety Champagne with soft, fruity aromas. It was
very balanced on the palate and golden in color, feeling
perfectly in tune with the sunshine that flooded the farm.

Adèle looked a lot like Simone Signoret from the
film *The Widow Couderc* from 1971 and had a distinct
Parisian accent. She showered them with cold cuts, freshly
baked flatbreads, and cheeses. Tommaso was very
impressed with the *Crottin de Chavignon*, a delectable goat's
cheese with a slight aftertaste of dried fruit, and the *Buche
de Sainte-Maure de Touraine*, a white and soft type of cheese
wrapped in a crisp, bluish rind. Julie's grandmother did not

hold back on sweets either. She served *Palet Solognot* (butter cookies with raisins), *Tarte Tatin*, and the ubiquitous *Madeleines*. After feasting, the four friends were taken on a tour of the vineyards.

In addition to the rows of the more well-known and unfailing Chardonnay and Pinot Noir, they also recognized several rows of Arbanne and Petit Meslier. Enjoying the fresh air and warm sunshine, they listened to the elderly couple, indulging in the musicality and sweetness of their words. Julie walked ahead of the group, holding her grandmother's hand, looking more like a happy child.

Returning from the walk, after settling down on a deck chair on the veranda, Tommaso had the impression that every single muscle in his body was relaxed. He wondered if it was time to turn on his phone but left it off so as not to risk ruining the state of bliss he was in. Bertrand, noticing that he was quiet, kept filling his glass with the consideration of someone accustomed to taking care of his guests. Meanwhile, he never interrupted his pleasant discourse that Tommaso perceived as a French-viticultural variant of Muzak background music, to which the boy decided to drift off, stretching his legs on the armchair and closing his eyes.

A sudden rumble woke him up fifteen minutes later. A young man had just parked a large Japanese motorcycle at the end of the gravel driveway. After he placed his helmet on the ground, he hugged Julie with the affection that only long-term acquaintance and genuine affection could elicit. Roberta, who sat beside him, filled him in.

"That's Arnaud, the neighbor's son. He's a lifelong family friend, as I understand it. I think he's quite handsome. I might settle here."

Tommaso watched Julie walk away with the boy and felt a tinge of jealousy. He then smiled to himself and tapped his pants pocket, touching his smartphone. His treasure was there. Once again, he was surprised at how the perspective of things around him could change so quickly.

That trip was becoming a true kaleidoscope of emotions. With each turn of the knob, things fragmented and then reassembled into different and increasingly more fascinating shapes. The purchase of the bottle was proving to be a sort of catalyst—although admittedly an expensive one—with unpredictable repercussions.

Dinner was on par with the snack they were served earlier. Once again, Adèle revealed her impressive cooking skills, preparing several scrumptious dishes. The cordial atmosphere and the wine made Julie's linguistic mediation unnecessary, and she gladly gave up being a translator for her friends. In the large room on the first floor, enlivened by the burning fireplace, the young girl's grandparents established themselves as excellent hosts. Bertrand told amusing anecdotes while Adèle took turns asking Tommaso and Luciano a few questions, thus making them feel like they were at center stage. After dinner, weary and happy, they all retreated to their respective rooms.

Just before crawling into bed, Tommaso heard the sound of a motorcycle. Attempting not to make noise, he opened the window shutters ajar and peeked out. He saw Arnaud on the driveway, wearing a leather jacket. A moment later, Julie joined him, slipping on her helmet and sitting behind him on the motorcycle. Tommaso stood watching them as they rode away. When the headlights faded into the night, he closed the shutters. He lay in bed with his phone off in his hand, feeling conflicted and undecided about what to do.

I can't be afraid of my own phone!

Finally, he switched on his phone, worrying that Sara could have replied to his message and interpreted his silence as a lack of interest on his part. He held his breath for a few seconds, feeling ridiculous about his own fears.

How bad can it be? Worst comes to worst, she didn't reply.

He thought that with a hint of superstition, trusting that he'd find a text message from the girl. He imagined what her message would say and pictured himself upon his return to Rome, intent on telling her every detail about his adventurous trip, made timeless by the conquest of the coveted bottle.

As he switched on his phone, the notifications came rolling in. They appeared on the smartphone display in the following order: Mail, Social media, Messenger, and finally, WhatsApp.

There it was, Sara's text!

The preview seemed promising to him.

It stated, "Beautiful! I envy you."

He clicked on the box to read the full message but found nothing more.

"Beautiful! I envy you."

That was it. Nothing more.

What seemed like the beginning of a conversation headed in the right direction turned out to be a painful mockery in a split second.

He reread those short words several times until they began to dance before his eyes. He left the app and opened it again a moment later, though he knew he would find nothing else. Dejected, he laid the phone on the bed sheets and laughed at himself.

What did he expect, though? Sara had been kind to him, but that did not mean she was interested. As a matter of fact, she had not said or done anything that would entitle him to think she felt emotionally involved.

He sighed, concluding that he had most likely projected the reflection of his desire onto her. Despite the stinging disappointment, he realized that, after all, he did not mind that he had fooled himself. Hope indeed had been sweet. Moreover, if he could have gone back, he would have done the same things, nurturing the same hopes.

He tried to get distracted and found himself thinking about Julie. He wondered what she was up to with the handsome Arnaud. His mind went back to what happened—or rather what did not happen—in the galleries of the Veuve Clicquot cellars. He wondered if he had missed an opportunity but told himself that he had not.

Julie was only a friend. A very good friend. Even though he was a little jealous of the French dude who had taken her away like a knight on his horse.

He touched the phone with his finger. That device represented his very slender and virtual connection to Sara (if one could call it that). Exhausted by those thoughts, he fell asleep after a few minutes.

CHAPTER 23

"Wine and man remind me of two wrestlers who are friends,
who fight each other relentlessly, and continually make peace.
The vanquished always embraces the victor."
Charles Baudelaire

In the dark, lost in the French countryside in Julie's grandparents' vineyard, he could not find his way back to his bedroom. He was not frightened but worried that he would not get enough rest for the trip the following day. It made no sense to be out in the vineyard late at night. He could not even remember why he had gone out. It was insane. How could he be so irresponsible at his age? Maybe he should have gone home, back to Italy. Did he notify the office about his absence? He could not remember. Perhaps if he had set off at a good pace, he would have been able to get to the office within a few hours. Too bad he couldn't see farther than his nose. In that dark, he would have risked wandering around all night. However, the house could not have been too far away. After all, he had walked all the way there, and it did not take him that long, as far as he remembered.

He was not surprised when he found himself driving his car.

Evidently, he must have parked it nearby. He caught a glimpse of some street signs in the darkness. The markings were faded and fuzzy, but he was quite sure of the direction to follow. Maintaining proper control of the car, however, was difficult. The steering wheel had become inexplicably hard, and the brakes were not working. On top of that, the road lighting was dim, and some areas were completely dark.

He saw a sign flash by his side, pointing in the direction of Rome.

He promised himself he would take the next turn. Another signpost appeared, yet again indicating the way to Rome, except this time, it pointed in the opposite direction. He was not surprised. He was sure an old saying claimed all roads lead to Rome, even when they were supposed to take you elsewhere. He thought going to London had been only an illusion, and no road would ever lead them there. Their bottle would be waiting for them in Rome.

At one point, the car began to pick up speed. There was no longer asphalt under the tires but dirt and grass. The landscape around him turned dull gray, and the images blurred. The steering wheel was now unresponsive, so he turned his attention to the brakes. The car skidded on the uneven ground until, slowly, it finally stopped. A large wooden door appeared in front of him.

He got out of the car and realized he was standing in front of a Gothic church, surrounded by the desolate countryside. At that moment, as if a lightning flash had struck him, he realized that inside that church, he would be able to solve the mystery of that trip, which involved the very essence of wine, its nature, and its endless metaphors.

He did not understand how, but now he found himself indoors.

It was daylight, and sunlight cloaked the aisles in a diffused glow through the stained glass windows. As he looked around, he understood that the key to the enigma lay in the clues suggested by the sacred images, the venerable furnishings, and the symbolism of each dusty relic.

An old priest dressed as a sommelier emerged from the altar.

Here's someone who can help me! Tommaso thought.

"Forgive me, Father, for I am ignorant. I need notions of art history to unravel this enigma. And I don't have them."

The old priest smiled graciously at him.

"It depends on what you're looking for. Some secrets lie within us."

Tommaso remained silent, and the priest shrugged his shoulders.

"Unless, of course, we're talking about mysteries like that of the Templars or, even more unfathomable, that of the Holy Grail..."

"What can I do, then?"

"First, you have to figure out what you're looking for."

He did not know. He only remembered that he had left to buy a bottle of wine. He told the priest, fearing that piece of information might upset him.

To his surprise, the old man understood and nodded.

"Then we'll have to look thoroughly around here."

Tommaso began to inspect the church. He could only distinguish a few details, such as goldwork, render, the outlines of a few carvings, moldy drapes, or the worn edges of ancient sarcophaguses, so he merely followed the priest, who was talking to himself, listing each item he examined.

After a long unsuccessful search, the priest scratched his chin thoughtfully.

"We are looking in the wrong place. Where could one find wine? Certainly not anywhere in the nave."

Hearing the priest's words, Tommaso had an epiphany.

"Maybe we should look in the tabernacle!"

The old man nodded vigorously.

"Sure, that makes sense. Then I know where to go."

He waved a finger, indicating him to follow. Tommaso found himself in a dark, cramped-up, rock-walled crawlspace, squelched by an unpleasant sense of claustrophobia. To his surprise, suddenly, that damp gully opened out into a large dungeon lit by artificial lights. It was clean and gleaming, filled with mirrors and chromium-plated fittings. An altar was in the center, covered with a tablecloth. On it were food, bottles, and glasses. A loud and colorful crowd moved around the table, chatting and having an aperitif.

No one paid any attention to them. Not at all surprised by the change of scene, the old priest moved casually through the hustle and bustle.

A guy in a tuxedo approached him, smiling complacently.

"I know why you came here. You're looking for a woman."

He wasn't, though the idea of disappointing him displeased him.

"Actually, I'm looking for a bottle of wine."

The man elbowed him.

"Aren't they the same thing?"

Two altar boys standing behind the buffet signaled for him to come closer. Skillfully exchanging duties, they quickly made him a cocktail. When he tried to drink it, he noticed the liquid was murky, filled with small chips and other impurities. Trying to be inconspicuous, he put the glass in his pocket and reached for the priest, who was fiddling at the head of the table with the tabernacle. When the priest managed to open it, it turned out to be empty.

At that moment, he got an idea. He took the glass from his pocket and placed it in the tabernacle. It fitted perfectly. The priest looked at him, showing gratitude.

Suddenly, everyone stopped talking and turned to look at him. A long and roaring applause followed. Everyone was over the moon and seemed to have understood something fundamental.

Yes, everyone had finally understood the solution to the riddle.

Everyone except him.

CHAPTER 24

"Nothing makes the future look so rosy as to contemplate it through a glass of Chambertin."
Napoleon Bonaparte

The early morning light brought an end to that absurd dream. It was not easy for Tommaso, Roberta, and Luciano to say goodbye to Bertrand and Adèle. Partly because they had gotten along so well, but mostly because Bertrand and Adèle perfectly embodied the life they longed so much to live, and yet due to age, chance, or choice, they were denied that life (at least for the time being).

Julie's eyes were a little tired, and she was visibly emotional when she hugged her grandparents goodbye. After taking a group photo, the friends hopped into the car. Before leaving, they received a farewell gift from the couple: a basket filled with goodies such as sandwiches, fruit, and a few bottles of wine. "We should take trips like this more often," said Roberta, beaming as soon as Tommaso started the engine.

"I can't remember who said that 'one goes on a journey only to leave something behind,' but the longer I'm away, the less I feel attached to what I left behind," she added, chuckling to make it clear that she didn't mean it. Well, not entirely, at least.

"I also feel like I'm changing too quickly," confirmed Tommaso. "If things keep going this way, by the time I get back to the firm, my partner won't recognize me."

"Would that be such a bad thing?" asked Julie without opening her eyes, dozing off in the back seat.

"Let's stop this philosophical moment here," Roberta intervened. "Let's get back to focusing on the goal and set a course to London without delay to pick up our bottle! Are you with me?"

Howls and cheers filled the vehicle. As the farm gradually became a distant speck behind them through the rearview mirror, Tommaso noticed that Julie had reopened her eyes. She was looking intensely at the house and vineyard as if she wanted to imprint them permanently in her memory.

After they stopped for lunch at a roadside inn, they arrived in Coquelles in the early afternoon. It began to rain as if the weather intended to emphasize that they were leaving *Douce France* (aka sweet France as per the Charles Trenet song) to land in misty England.

Boarding operations were relatively fast. They quickly found a place to park the car inside the shuttle of the Channel Tunnel. Unlike on a ferry, where one can park the car in the garage and then go on the deck, in the Channel Tunnel, one cannot leave the carriage. However, one can choose to either sit and relax in the car or walk along the sidewalk of the shuttle. After taking turns going to the restroom and considering the short duration of the crossing, they decided to get comfortable in the car.

"Can you imagine? We're about to disembark in London. We're one step away from our destination! What are we doing tonight?" asked Luciano.

"Maybe we should rest to show up sharp at the auction," replied Tommaso.

"You're crazy!" protested Roberta. "We are about to arrive in *Swinging London,* and you want to go to bed early?"

"Aside from the fact that your *Swinging London* has been dead for fifty years," Luciano teased her, "aren't you the one in charge of curbing our expenses?"

"Limit the budget, sure. But we didn't come all this way to fast and repent for our sins!"

"Actually, I don't feel like I've fasted at all so far," laughed Julie, dropping the melancholy that had accompanied her during the last few hours of the trip. "I've gained at least a couple of kilos in the last three days."

"All right, here's what we'll do," said Roberta. "Let's get to the hotel, rest a bit, take a quick shower, and then get back on track. How about a quiet, monastic dinner tonight to cleanse our palettes before the event?"

Roberta's suggestion was discarded with a shower of booing and joking whistles.

"If I liked monastic dinners, I would have become a nun," replied Julie.

"Come on, we're in London for a probably once-in-a-lifetime occasion, and you suggest prayers and repentance? I veto that."

"Me too," said Luciano.

"We don't want to be remembered as cloistered drinkers," rejoined Julie. "London is calling!"

Roberta looked at Tommaso for support.

"Which team are you in? With the prudent ants or the jolly cicadas?"

Tommaso, knee-deep in Hamletic doubt about whether or not to take a picture of the wagon to send to Sara, shrugged his shoulders.

"Considering that this trip takes me away for once from the pragmatic dimension of my life and into a decidedly more Dionysiac one, I think I will join the cicada team this time."

Roberta crossed her arms over her chest and put on a playful pout.

"Well, well, look at what a gang of epicureans I've gone and gotten involved with! All right, then, what do you guys suggest?"

Overwhelmed by having to come up with suggestions, the others remained silent before each tried to come up with a winning idea. It was not easy, partly because Roberta enjoyed rejecting each idea with sadistic pleasure.

A snack in a quaint English pub?

Nonsense! Quaint English pubs are everywhere. There must be at least 20 in Rome alone.

A trip to Piccadilly Circus?

What an original idea! No one would have thought of that. Let's go there, but then what? Are we going to camp there all night? Come on! You can do better than that.

Maybe a ride on the London Eye?

Oh, imagine that. A Ferris wheel, a sideshow, and an adult ride.

Intimidated by the single-minded determination with which Roberta was gradually crushing their suggestions, and perhaps more to unblock the situation than out of real conviction, Tommaso threw out what he had in mind.

"Mousetrap," he said.

The group went quiet.

"You mean the play based on the Agatha Christie novel?" asked Julie after a few seconds, rummaging through her memory.

"Just that one, a real London miracle. You can't find that one in Rome, Roberta. And, if I'm not mistaken, it's been going continuously for a long time. Fifty years and more, I would say."

This time the friend was not ready to retort.

"I've heard of it," Luciano commented. "I haven't read many Christie books. It's a detective novel, right?"

"Of course, it's a detective novel, you dummy!" Roberta teased him amicably. "Agatha Christie was the queen of detective novels!"

"All right. What's it about?"

"That I don't know."

"Smartphones out, children. Let's get to the bottom of this."

The Wi-Fi was working inside the shuttle, to everyone's surprise.

"A stormy evening," read Tommaso, "in a country hotel ... a crime... Gee, it's like one of my nightmares!"

"What nightmares?" asked Julie.

" One day, I will tell you about it. Now let's think about our friend Agatha, the mystery writer..."

"Very British," replied Roberta. "Is it still running? I mean, it's been going on for so long..."

"Yes," confirmed Tommaso. "It's sort of an institution now. It will go on until the end of time."

"And we could contribute to the legend," Julie added. "Taking a breather and getting reorganized before the battle is a pretty good idea. I'm in."

"Calm down. We'll have to call to see if there are tickets available," pointed out Tommaso. "But that's fine with me. Luciano, what about you?"

"I'm in your hands, children. So far, it hasn't gone too badly for me, I must admit."

Tommaso seemed to discern a fleeting glimpse of understanding between Luciano and Roberta, but because the direct lights created a deceptive glare inside the car, he was not sure.

Fortunately, the St. Martin's Theater website was easy to navigate. When they selected the evening performance scheduled for that same day, a floor plan opened up with the available seats. They chose the so-called stalls, a few rows away from the stage.

"We found four good seats," remarked Tommaso, "but the tickets cost one hundred pounds each."

Roberta, true to her role as the group's treasurer, illustrated a quick cost-benefit ratio of the evening to her friends. However, she could not keep a straight face for too long.

"I warn you that Agatha will cost us four hundred pounds out of our joint budget. In addition, we will also have to eat something..."

Before the friends could even air their thoughts, it was the woman herself who ended the conversation.

"Look, you've convinced me. I, too, have been itching for a night at the theater with dear old Aunt Agatha. Right now, I can't imagine anything more English. So yes, let's do it. But let's not forget why we came all this way."

Tommaso confirmed the tickets and purchased them online. They studied the area together and checked out available public transportation to get from the hotel to Covent Garden, where the theater was.

Each day brought out new stimuli and new destinations. The Romanée-Conti was always on Tommaso's mind, but perhaps it was no longer the number one priority.

CHAPTER 25

*"I like dark corners in sleeping taverns, where people peak in excess of singing;
I like blasphemous light things and deep wine glasses, in which the mind rejoices,
reaching a level of magical thinking."*
Alda Merini

Locked in that shuttle, somewhat reminiscent of a spaceship, Tommaso did not perceive any movement and compared the journey under the English Channel to teleportation.

When they disembarked at Cheriton, it was cold and rainy, and the sky was dark. After a stop for gas and a snack, they resumed their journey. It took them an hour and a half to reach London and another forty-five minutes to navigate the city traffic. Their hotel was in a very classy-looking residential area within walking distance of Saint James Park, one of the capital's many parks. The building was on the corner of two streets, with an imposing facade developed over three floors and an entrance flanked by two large windows with tinted glass panes. Its large and bright sign lured them in. Reaching their destination had been a tour de force that would have exhausted even the most expert travelers. Nevertheless, although the journey had slightly worn them out, they reached their respective rooms, took a refreshing shower, and met back in the lobby, united by their mission and ready for the evening.

The air was cold, but at least it was no longer raining. Tommaso would have liked to have more time to enjoy the city, interpret and internalize it, but he knew their schedule did not allow it. Piccadilly Circus, one of London's many beating hearts (as highlighted in every city guide), greeted him with its huge glowing screens. Perhaps they had once been a spectacle, but at that moment, he only saw them as a magnified version of the many screens that ruled his and every person's life. Somewhat dazed by the chaos of the crowd, he wandered with his friends around the square until they found shelter on the steps of the famous Shaftesbury Memorial Fountain.

Keeping their windbreakers closed tight, the four friends huddled shoulder to shoulder in an attempt to shield themselves from the cold and humidity and perhaps also to find comfort in each other's presence amid that confusing blend of sounds and people. After a few minutes in that position, Julie broke the silence.

"Guys, what are we doing here?"

"We are enjoying Piccadilly Circus," Luciano promptly replied.

They all burst out laughing.

"I say let's get up and move. I can't stay still for much longer," the girl urged them.

They took the tube and headed for Covent Garden.

Tommaso felt like he was moving slower than everything else around him. Ideas, assessments, or even simple sensations seemed to struggle to cross his mind, and even when they finally landed, it was already time to see and reflect on something else.

I need to take a break. When this is over, I have to take stock of the situation.

By then, Sara occupied a well-defined space in his mind. Whatever he was doing or thinking, her image hovered over his subconscious. He wished he could have shared every moment with her.

I really did change.

They arrived at Covent Garden fairly early. St. Martin's Theatre was smaller than they had expected, which made it look even more seductive. It looked like something out of a novel, with a large neon sign shining on the wall that read, "Agatha Christie's The Mousetrap."

They entered and checked their reservations. The lobby was intimate and looked like it had been immune to the passage of time. On one wall, a wooden panel informed the public that the theater was close to reaching twenty-eight thousand performances. After collecting their tickets, they stopped by the colorful souvenir stand. Roberta purchased a bag with mice drawn on it, Julie a sweatshirt with a print depicting fingerprints, and Tommaso and Luciano bought T-shirts that read "Suspect everyone." Tommaso's friends noticed that the T-shirt he chose was a size XS, but no one mentioned it.

They still had a full hour before the show, so they took advantage of the wait and had a light dinner at a bar next door. The place was packed, and the several big TVs kept at high volume made communication difficult.

"We catapulted from the quiet French countryside to the chaos of your *swinging London* without even a moment to gather our thoughts. To say I'm dazed is an understatement," Luciano complained, turning to Roberta.

Julie nodded.

"The world has gotten awfully small. There used to be plenty of time to ease into the new environments—enough to even get tired of them. Right now, however, I can barely realize where I am..."

"Don't worry, children," Roberta tried to cheer them up. "We'll relax and have fun this evening. It's our chance to recharge our batteries in anticipation of the big battle that awaits us in two days. We'll enjoy the theater, then maybe have a chat in a quieter place, and finally go to the hotel to get a good night's sleep."

Inside, the theater was small, all wood and velvet. Photographs of the actors who had played the various parts over the years were hung on the wall near the entrance. Tommaso found them disturbing. It felt like watching the passage of time, and a strange anxiety arose deep within him. He felt the need to do *something*. Something true, something important, something real, while he still had the time. Just as on that wall, newer faces had replaced those who came before them; someone would, sooner or later, take his place in the spotlight of life.

The theater was full. Tommaso sat next to Julie, Luciano, and Roberta.

"Does anyone know who the murderer is?" asked Luciano.

No one knew.

"Honestly," Julie admitted, "The only thing I know about Agatha Cristie's work is *Murder on the Orient Express*. I saw it at the movie theater, and I liked it."

"I think I've read all her books," Roberta intervened. "Miss Marple, Poirot, her short stories... For a while, when I was alone after work, in the evening, all I did was read— mostly detective stories. I was coming out of a long, very troubled relationship, and I couldn't stand sentimental books or movies. So I threw myself into mystery novels. They became like a protective bubble that sheltered me from my daily anxieties. Tonight's show will be like a reunion."

Luciano squeezed her arm confidentially.

"Admit it. You are only pretending not to remember who the murderer is because you want to surprise us by revealing their identity right before they disclose it."

"Oh, come on. Although... I could spoil it..."

They did not even let her finish, jokingly reprimanding her.

The secluded hotel in the snow, the characters and their ambiguity, the growing intensity—the first half absorbed them completely. Everyone in the lobby was very excited, and the friends used the intermission to compare their theories and suspicions about how the plot would unfold. They tried to get hints from Roberta, but she did not give anything away, almost feeling sympathy for those amateurs playing detective. An hour later, when the plot was approaching its final twist, Julie's left hand and Tommaso's right hand touched. It happened naturally, and they did not feel any need to say anything to each other. They found comfort in discovering they were so similar and also so alone right when someone came into their lives.

No one guessed the murderer, but as they walked out of the theater and into the cold city streets, they all swore they had their suspicions about the culprit from the beginning but kept quiet so as not to ruin the surprise for the others.

"What were you saying about your nightmares?" Julie asked Tommaso all of a sudden.

"Nothing much. It's just that since this whole business about the bottle started, my dreams have been full-on cinematic."

"Tell us about them!" urged Roberta, holding his arm.

"Sorry to disappoint you. Not today!"

"Then when?" teased Luciano.

"Maybe when we get back to Rome."

"Don't act all mysterious now!" insisted Julie. "We are your best friends, and we demand to know about your nightly delusions, especially if they involve us."

"Nein!" remarked Tommaso as he started running down the sidewalk. "You won't get me, cops!"

Julie was the first to play along and went after him. Luciano and Roberta burst out laughing and joined in immediately behind them.

"They're going to arrest us for disorderly conduct!" Roberta shouted, but Tommaso was already too far ahead. "Guys, I think we'll go back to the hotel. We are not that young anymore! If you two want to stay downtown and hang out a little longer, go ahead. I'm exhausted."

"Be good, mind you," Luciano added, winking at them.

"What do you think? Should we also go to sleep?" Julie inquired Tommaso.

"I'm tired too, but I'd like to walk around some more. I love this city so much, and I rarely come here. It feels like breathing a different world."

"Then I'll keep you company. I'm a little sleepy, but I can handle walking a few more kilometers."

Tommaso and Julie said goodnight to their friends and started walking toward Soho. They ordered two Rusty Nails at *Termini Bar*, a tiny place in the style of Italian clubs from the 1960s, with deliberately old-fashioned decor and a great selection of cocktails and long drinks. The small tables were all taken, so they sat on the stools at the counter. Tommaso ordered some appetizers.

"So, tell me about this Sara."

Julie looked at him, smiling as if that was the most ordinary topic in the world for a casual conversation.

"There's not much to tell, really. I really like her. I'd be lying if I said the opposite—but I barely know her. I don't even know if she has a boyfriend or a fiancé."

"I see, but what do you think when you are with her? How are you, and how is she? You can tell if someone isn't having a good time or if they are not fully there because they'd rather be with someone else."

"I don't get to spend time with her often. In fact, it's pretty rare. But when I do, I feel good. I'm always a little nervous, but my feelings are positive, and I wouldn't want to leave. I feel the same when I'm with you, though."

"Do I make you nervous?" she asked him, surprised.

"No, you don't make me nervous. Not on purpose, anyway. I'm just shy, that's all."

"What about Sara?"

"What about her?"

"What is she like when you're together? Does she go out of her way to dump you there and leave early? Is she impatient and looks at her smartphone all the time? Or does she stare into your eyes while you're talking, smiling constantly and laughing at your jokes? Does she touch your arm or hand while you chat?"

Tommaso shook his head and laughed.

"I don't know. Why are you girls like this? You make us feel awkward. You always want to know everything! We don't know how to respond..."

"Tommy, be honest."

"I think she enjoys my company. There, I said it. Are you happy now? She laughs, smiles, touches my arm, and I always get the impression that she's trying to find an excuse to stay a little longer—or that she wants to see me again soon."

"It's a done deal then."

"It's not done at all. She doesn't show up at my place on her motorcycle to pick me up, Julie. She doesn't take any initiative. That's why I have my doubts. Sometimes it seems like she's letting herself go a little more, then the next time, she's back to being composed and serious, acting a lot more distant. I don't know what's going on, believe me."

"What if she's shy too?" she suggested, pinching his cheek with her fingers. "You didn't consider that, huh?"

"I don't know. Let's just pay and go, shall we?"

"All right. Let's take a walk."

They went out. The air had become stinging cold, so they clung to each other. Not far away, they saw the bright *Trade Soho* sign.

"What do you say, shall we go there?"

"Let's ask how much admission costs and then decide," Tommaso replied. He asked two girls standing at the front door for info. After revealing to him the entrance fee, the girls suggested all four of them go in together. They said their names were Lara Jane and Suzie. They studied ancient literature and loved to party in the evenings. The place looked like a basement, and it was cozy and warm. They drank two bottles of Champagne, then felt the need to get out to get some fresh air again, so they took another walk to scout the area.

"So, do you have a crush on that guy with the motorcycle? The French guy?"

"What are you talking about, Tom? We're just friends."

"Give me a break. I've seen you going through the vineyards late at night..."

"All right. It was just a slip-up. It happens, right?"

Laughing, they walked into a place called *El Camion*. The environment was lively and colorful, inviting them to have fun. They got drinks, and Julie, despite being tired, started dancing. Tommaso stayed seated at the bar and watched her, enchanted by the sense of freedom and inner peace she exuded. It was turning out to be a truly beautiful and liberating evening he would surely remember. He felt alive and invincible, even uninhibited, as he had rarely ever felt in his life.

That was why he decided to go for it when a beautiful girl named Gilly approached the bar and ordered the same cocktail he was drinking while giving him a nod.

After all, what's wrong with letting myself go a little for once? Even if I make a fool of myself, I will never see this girl again.

A moment later, he was dancing with her. The club was noisy, and they spoke very little, but she made it clear that she was engaged.

After an hour or so, Julie suggested they went to the casino and asked Gilly to come along. She was feeling lucky that night and wanted to try to win back the money she spent on drinks—and maybe even earn something extra. In the end, they did not win anything and stopped testing their luck before they went completely broke. Tommaso did not mind when Gilly disappeared as suddenly as she had appeared. Julie let him know that some guy named Robert had come to pick her up.

They left the casino at dawn. The tube was full of commuters going to work out of town, and Julie and Tommaso felt exhausted and guilty. They managed to find two seats and fell asleep with their heads resting against the glass. The train stopped abruptly, awakening Julie, who tugged Tommaso by his sleeve.

"Tom, I think we missed our stop. We have to get off and go back."

"Sorry for leaving you by yourself earlier."

"What?"

"Yeah, I mean, I danced with that girl and..."

"What's wrong with that? Tommy, you worry too much, really. Let's go."

They got off and walked through the tunnel leading in the other direction. They were glad to find that the compartment was half-empty. Lulled by the gentle movement of the vehicle, Tommaso fell asleep again. Julie rested her head on his shoulder and closed her eyes.

When they arrived at the hotel, it was almost eight o'clock in the morning (they missed their stop twice more). Without saying another word, they went to sleep.

CHAPTER 26

"More important than the food pairing is the person with whom you drink the wine"
Christian Moueix

The next day, the four friends followed their itinerary as planned. They visited the most interesting places but began to feel tired from all the kilometers they traveled. Tommaso and Julie, who still felt a bit shaken by the long night out, did not tell their traveling mates anything about the time they spent together.

That evening, after going to different clubs, they stopped at a small park. They thought they should celebrate their second night in London properly before returning to the hotel. After all, they had the entire following morning to rest. They postponed taking the tube and walked around. The air was fresh and pleasant, and the lights and people surrounding them triggered their senses, kindling their attention.

They walked in silence, side by side, letting the flow of the crowd carry them along as if they were on a raft abandoned to lazy sea currents. Julie nonchalantly held Tommaso's arm—a gesture devoid of subtext, relaxing for both of them. Whenever Julie noticed something, she squeezed his elbow, and he reacted by contracting his muscles. Roberta and Luciano walked a couple of meters ahead and kept laughing like kids.

They reached St. Paul's Cathedral, with its imposing eighteenth-century facade lit by several lights. They stopped to watch a few street performers, then proceeded to Waterloo Bridge on the River Thames. There, they took some pictures and immediately sent them to different people. Each of them had someone they brought with them on that trip in one way or another. After that, they gathered on a bench.

Luciano consulted his watch.

"I don't know about you, but all this walking has made me hungry. How about we get something to eat before going to bed?"

"I'm also hungry. Also, a sip of good wine wouldn't hurt," Roberta backed him up.

"We didn't come here to smoke just half a cigar," Julie announced, surprising everyone. Her friends gave her a confused look. "I can't remember what novel it's from, but I thought it was an appropriate analogy," she explained, revealing that she was quoting that figure of speech from a book.

"Right," Tommaso agreed. Sara was still constantly in his thoughts, and he needed a distraction. "Let's go smoke the other half of the cigar."

They did not want to give up the evening breeze by taking the tube, so once again, they walked. They went to Covent Garden, where there were many restaurants to choose from. After passing on a few overpriced ones, hungry and tired, they moved to a different area and headed for *Hedonism Wines*, a multi-story restaurant with large windows in Mayfair. Julie stopped to admire the long rows of crystal goblets hanging upside-down from long racks suspended below the ceiling, next to brick walls that were so adorably English.

"This place is great. I've been wanting to come here forever!"

Roberta ran her gaze along the countless shelves that housed hundreds of bottles divided by nationality, all cleverly accompanied by tags containing short descriptions and prices.

Tommaso had been in that restaurant a few years back, so he led the way.

The place was packed, so they considered it a miracle when the waiter took them to a table near the window that had just become available. Once seated, Luciano offered to take the lead.

"I say we start by trying a wine from the *wine dispenser.* What do you think?"

The two men opted for a glass of *This is not an exit* from *Sine Qua Non,* a renowned California winery. Their wines cost a fortune, and the waiting list to visit them is years long.

"They have a *Syrah made* with a small portion of other French grapes. Have you ever tasted it, Luciano? I'd be curious to hear what aromas you recognize in this wine."

"I'm sorry to disappoint you, but I won't satisfy your curiosity tonight," his friend replied, surprising him. "You see, trying to describe a great wine through a series of scents can be the equivalent of talking about a person by merely listing what they wear rather than speaking about their character."

In the meantime, Julie and Roberta got a bottle of *2011 Nyetimber Blanc de blancs* to drink on the spot. They asked the staff to bring something to go with the wines.

Pretty soon, the group started feeling the effect of the alcohol, combined with fatigue and the heat of the restaurant. Julie's cheeks were red, and Luciano gave a long speech about how London was during its roaring years, with miniskirts, the Beatles, and Highgate ghost hunters. He touched on different topics incoherently based on his friends' questions and amused comments. A waiter brought them appetizers just as Luciano was sharing an anecdote about Twiggy, the famous model whose name is forever linked to the history of the miniskirt. After the men finished their glasses of wine, Julie and Roberta shared their bottle with them.

As he drank, Tommaso noticed that his perception of the past and future was beginning to fade. Relieved but also a bit worried, he realized that the present occupied all his attention. It was a strange feeling but not at all unpleasant. The wine was great, and Luciano and Roberta were competing to mention names and events from *Swinging London* while Julie intervened to ask for details or make jokes. The background noise of the wine shop (voices, the clatter of cutlery, footsteps, chairs being moved, doors opening and closing) isolated them from the rest of the world. The long walk had awakened their appetite, and now they had let go of all their restraint. Roberta, frequently leaning her shoulder against Luciano's, was busy praising the (alleged) glory of that unique era. It did not take long before even Tommaso joined that frenzy of names, anecdotes, and places.

It was finally time for dessert. Tommaso looked at his friends, and it was clear to him that they, too, wished they never had to get up from that table and that oasis of pure peace, cut out from the raw daily routine of their existence. The restaurant, which earlier was filled with customers of the most diverse nationalities, began to empty, and soon they were left alone. It almost surprised them when the waiter arrived at their table with the bill.

Roberta gasped when she looked at it, remembering only at that moment that she was supposed to keep track of the group's spending. The wine and cheerfulness of the last few hours made her forget her role.

"Well, in London, in a place like this, these are the prices," she exclaimed after a second, interrupting the silence that had since fallen at the table. "I had a good time and ate even better. As Edith Piaf would have said, *Je ne regrette rien.*"

"That may be so, but I think *Swinging London* just gave us a good beating," Luciano commented, less convinced.

Once outside, the cold hit them hard. The evening breeze had turned into an icy wind, with heavy rain starting to fall from the sky. They would have gotten soaked wet if they had taken the tube, so they called a cab. They did not say a word during the car ride, partly because they were tired but also because they were pondering what consequences that enjoyable evening might have on the following day's auction. One thing was certain, their chances of winning had dwindled. They needed a lot of luck to win the bottle. That was still on their mind as they went to their respective rooms. They all felt guilty, as if they had broken a commitment or betrayed mutual trust. More than losing the Romanée-Conti, Tommaso was worried about how awkward he would have felt having to admit to Sara that the bottle escaped him twice. Julie, probably sensing what was going through her friend's head, gently squeezed his arm.

"Don't be too upset about it. It's not worth it. It's just a bottle of wine. There will be other occasions anyway."

Tommaso appreciated his friend's words, but they were not enough to make him feel better. Luciano's expression revealed he was clearly disappointed and angry, making it hard not to feel uncomfortable when crossing his gaze. He was aware that he could not blame any of them for that turn of events since he was the one who suggested letting loose that evening. Yet he could not seem to come to terms with what happened. Roberta, for her part, seemed more surprised by how everything could change so drastically in just a couple of hours.

"I'm tired, and I'm having a hard time thinking straight. I need to sleep. I'll see you in the morning for breakfast. Let's not worry too much about the math now. It's pointless."

Back in the room, while Luciano took a shower, Tommaso looked at the pictures he had taken that evening. Finally, he shrugged his shoulders and sent them to Sara. After all, what did he have to lose?

After sleeping for a few hours, a cramp in his right calf woke him up. He felt restless and sweaty. He looked at the clock. It was just after five in the morning. In the bed next to him, Luciano was still sleeping soundly. He went to the bathroom and rinsed his face with cold water, then lay down again, trying to fall back asleep. He tossed and turned restlessly in bed but eventually gave up. He turned on his cell phone and checked the website of the *67 Pall Mall*, a fancy, world-famous club renowned for its exclusive wines they would be visiting in a few hours.

Looking at the pictures, he gradually felt sleepy again, but before he switched off his phone, he scrolled through the chat with Sara and reread their previous conversations. They were normal. They looked like simple conversations between colleagues who maybe were not even friends. Suddenly, those dry, short messages seemed dry and devoid of any affection or involvement, and a sense of hopelessness enveloped him like a thorny blanket. Most probably, Sara saw him as a friendly colleague with whom to exchange small talk or perhaps have a drink and nothing more. All those times he thought he noticed a spark of interest in her eyes for something more than a friendship, he had been wrong. Now he was sure of that.

But what about Julie? How did he really see Julie? He did feel a bit jealous when he saw her ride away on a motorcycle with that handsome French guy. However, in all honesty, the feelings he had for Sara were not comparable to anything he had experienced with Julie in the winery, in the car, or her grandparents' vineyard.

Julie was beautiful, intelligent, and loved wine. She was wonderful. However, he had fallen hopelessly in love with the wrong woman.

Overwhelmed, he sank into a very heavy sleep.

CHAPTER 27

"Sometimes wine is the liquid manifestation of silence."
Luis Sepúlveda

The following morning, the four friends met for breakfast. None of them had slept well, and Tommaso noticed they also could not process what had happened the night before.

Indeed, what did happen? Quite simply, for the first time, they realized they had spent a good portion of the budget they had set aside to purchase the bottle, which was enough to spoil their mood. Their chances of winning the auction had dwindled and were now close to zero. Although, they did not lose their marbles and went on a spending spree. On the contrary, they actually stuck strictly to their travel plan and stayed within their budget. Yet they seemed mortified, especially Roberta, who—albeit humorously—had appointed herself as the group's treasurer. She looked like a lost soul. Tommaso felt compelled to boost the collective spirits.

"Listen to me carefully. Apart from the fact that nothing is lost yet, we came here essentially to take a trip together. Our bottle is the icing on the cake. If we bring it home, we will say, 'Mission accomplished.' However, it is an auction, and we have to consider that we might not win. It was a possibility even before we left. Sure, if we had been more careful with our spending and saved every penny, we could now count on a higher budget, but how much higher? We still wouldn't have enough money to enter the auction as sure winners. In fact, we never had any guarantees, but we still enjoyed the trip and did exactly what we wanted to do. If we had only sandwiches and beer during the trip, we would have missed out on many wonderful experiences."

"He's right!" exclaimed Julie, smiling again. "Besides, we're scheduled to visit the *67 Pall Mall Club* today, right? Well, it won't exactly be free. So what should we do? Should we give that up, hoping the money we save will make a difference at the auction? If that's what you want, then I'm with you. But is that really what you want?"

They stayed silent for a while. Finally, Luciano spoke up.

"The *Pall Mall* is one of the highlights of our trip. I mean, we wanted to go there together. For a wine enthusiast in London, it is a must-see. However, if you decide it's better not to go..."

His voice trailed off. Julie burst out laughing.

"There, you see? Let's not kid ourselves. We'd all be depressed if we skipped the *Pall Mall*. Let's fully enjoy the vacation, and then, later today, we'll see what happens! In any case, we will have no regrets."

Luciano regained his color.

"Well, if you put it that way, I agree."

Roberta, too, was glad to grab onto the life preserver Julie had tossed them.

"Then it's settled! It's just that I felt a little responsible. Last night I originally planned to watch my spending, but then..." He burst out laughing. "Oh my God, how much did we eat? And drink? When we were done with dinner, I thought I would never be able to get up from my chair!"

"Not to mention they practically had to throw us out," Tommaso added, feeling glad they were in a much better mood. "At one point, one of the waiters started circling our table like a vulture. He clearly couldn't wait for us to leave."

"I didn't notice that," Luciano said.

"Of course, you didn't notice!" teased Julie. "You were too busy drinking Champagne! When you go to Japan, you'll have to only eat raw fish and seaweed to get your shape back."

Tommaso felt relieved and thought the worst part was over. However, as they left the hotel and headed for the tube, he felt some tension was still in the air. It was understandable. Their showdown with the Romanée-Conti was approaching.

The introduction on the website read, *the 67 Pall Mall Club is located inside the magnificent building that once belonged to Sir Edwin Lutyens, in the heart of historic St James's. It offers one of the largest wine collections in London and also stores the members' own wines. Over time, it has become an institution for the wine industry and a landmark for the London social and food scene.*

Just before noon, they arrived in front of the building. The sun peeped through the clouds, casting blades of light and clusters of shadow on the structure. Standing in front of so much beauty—and what it represented—they realized they could have never skipped the visit.

They walked inside with the typical reverence of a visit to a temple. In a way, that was exactly what it was: a temple dedicated to wine and a certain lifestyle, Tommaso thought. He remembered reading that other English clubs did not treat their members the same way, with the same attention to small details that might seem incomprehensible or futile for commoners but were priceless to club members. For example, members could find freshly printed newspapers every morning, and coins and bills given to them as change were always brand-new.

Once they entered the airy, well-lit lobby, a waiter was appointed to show them around the club. He guided them to the bar, which was on par with the rest of the building. It had neoclassical friezes embellishing the top of the doors, light-colored walls decorated with period paintings and wall sconces, and a large mirror beyond the counter that made everything magically bright. The atmosphere was from another era, and modern tv screens and cash registers were the only visible connection to the present day.

The waiter explained that a meeting between retired army and navy officers was taking place. They were toasting and drinking White Ladies—a detail that contributed to that old-time vibe. The four friends sat at one of the marble tables, sinking into the soft leather armchairs. Tommaso speculated that "M" was among the former navy officers at that meeting.

"Who's "M"?" asked Roberta, intrigued.

"Don't tell me you've never heard of Admiral Miles Messervy, Commander of the Order of St. Michael and St. George and director of the British Secret Service, as well as James Bond's direct superior?"

Hearing those words, Julie instinctively turned around to look at the small group of elderly officers, trying to spot a familiar figure. A moment later, she realized how absurd that sounded.

"You're a fool," she dismissed her friend.

"All right, you caught me. 'M' doesn't exist," acknowledged Tommaso. "But if he did exist, he would surely come to a place like this. In fact, in Fleming's novels, M is a member of *Blades*. Although I believe that name is fictitious, his real-life equivalent may indeed be hiding among those elderly gentlemen."

One of them, wearing a Savile Row suit and regimental tie, realized he was the object of the group's attention. In response, he raised his glass to greet them.

"There, we're screwed! Your 'M' just caught us looking at him. He'll think we are Russian spies or something," exclaimed Roberta, amused and a little embarrassed at the same time.

"Don't worry. No Russian spy would ever be as clumsy as we are," Tommaso replied. "Besides, these are old-fashioned gentlemen. They would never bother us while we are tasting some good wine. Outside, maybe, but not here. They call it spiritual chivalry."

"Let's hope so," Luciano intervened. "I wouldn't want to end our trip in Guantánamo Bay."

"That would be the CIA's doing." Roberta teased him.

"So where do these people send their prisoners?"

"Maybe they don't send them anywhere. They just take them out."

"If they sent me to a place like this, I think I would turn myself in right away," Luciano concluded.

Tommaso felt refreshed by that exchange. At least they were in a good mood again. Sure, the uncertainty about the auction hovered over them like a sword of Damocles, but for the moment, the worst part was behind them. Perhaps that lingering sense of melancholy that he sensed in Julie's forced cheerfulness, Luciano's unusual lack of talkativeness, and even Roberta's sudden quietness were rooted in something else. Perhaps his friends were feeling incomplete—just like he was. The more their journey progressed, the more each of them probably wished they were in the company of someone who was more than just a friend.

There is nothing wrong with spending time with friends, of course. However, it is also natural to wish to share beautiful and meaningful moments with those at the center of our hearts, Tommaso thought.

He tried to look on the bright side. Having that experience with friends first might come in handy later, in case he wanted to revisit those places with... With whom? Tommaso realized that he was giving in to his fantasies again. If he kept thinking about Sara, he would only deceive himself further and suffer more. Yet he could picture taking her on that magnificent journey through Italy, France, and England, acting as her guide through the same itinerary he had already experienced, and seeing the joy and enthusiasm reflected in her eyes. The thought of that alone was enough to make him feel good.

A second waiter arrived at their table to show them the wine list on a tablet, thus interrupting his daydreaming. The wines were classified by place of origin, and the most numerous, predictably, were from France. There were so many that, for a moment, the four friends struggled to choose which ones to try. They found it easier to decide what to eat, but the choice of food was also less important. They did not want to feel too stuffed in the afternoon at the auction, so Tommaso and Roberta ordered roast beef and eggs Benedict while Julie and Luciano got omelets with ham, cheddar, mushrooms, and spinach. The meals were served with warm toasts on the side and accompanied by a bottle of Cécile Tremblay's Bourgogne Rouge.

They let the chatter of the clientele and the clinking of dishes and glasses lull them while they re-energized, making small talk and carefully avoiding mentioning the

Romanée-Conti. They concluded lunch with orange sorbet and coffee.

Luciano asked and managed to obtain permission to visit the underground cellar, where the Club stored its wine collection, as well as those of its members. The guide took them to a sort of vault containing thousands of bottles stored on shelves made of fine wood and glass. He explained that temperature and humidity were kept strictly in check, while the most insidious problem the technicians had to deal with was dust.

They left the Club with eyes full of wonder and returned to the hotel to freshen up in anticipation of the auction, which was scheduled to start at three o'clock. On the way back, feeling suspended between the pleasure they left at the *67 Pall Mall Club* and the fear of the upcoming battle, no one spoke. Tommaso would have liked to cheer his friends up but could not find the right words. He felt like a crusader who, arriving in the Holy Land after facing countless adversities, realizes he has left his sword at home.

CHAPTER 28

"Always ready for a new idea and an old wine."
Bertolt Brecht

An auction in a place as prestigious as Christie's was a new experience for all of them. When their cab stopped in front of the entrance, seeing the blue canopy with the house logo, they felt slightly intimidated. At that moment, Tommaso sensed he was about to face an unconquerable task. Julie squeezed his arm lightly to encourage him (but also to encourage herself).

Once inside, after showing their participation forms, they took the catalog and headed for the room indicated to them. They noticed that although they arrived early, many people were already there. The vibe in the room was more informal than they had expected, allowing Tommaso to ease the tension.

After all, it's just a place where they buy and sell fancy stuff, he thought.

Once they took their seats, he took a look around. The room's acoustics muffled the noise, and the white walls reflected the light that rained down from the tall screened windows and chandeliers.

The auctioneer's stand was positioned at the far end of the room, with a large digital screen behind showing the lot numbers and the bids with real-time conversion in different currencies. On either side were the compartments (many of them empty) from which operators could bid on behalf of the foreign clients with whom they were in contact over the phone.

Tommaso could sense his friends' excitement. While Luciano looked around discreetly, Roberta flipped through the catalog and seemed to be holding her breath. Sitting next to Tommaso, Julie had lost her usual boldness and looked like a child intimidated by unfamiliar surroundings.

"What time will they auction our Romanée-Conti?" she asked.

Roberta seemed taken aback.

"I saw you studying the catalog," she smiled at her.

"You're right. They have a lot of good stuff in here. Sorry, to tell you the truth, I'm a little overwhelmed by this place. So, let's see—here it is, it's lot seventy-eight."

"There are several bottles of DRC for auction from different vintages. There's even a 1945 Romanée-Conti," Luciano pointed out. "So maybe people won't pay too much attention to our 1991 Romanée-Conti, since it wasn't a particularly good year," he added, joking. Then, turning serious again, he shared his prophecy. "We will need a great deal of luck."

"*Audentes fortuna iuvat,*" recited Julie. "We've come this far, and now, we're on the battlefield. It's been a long journey, but I don't think we've done badly so far. Either way, we will defend our honor."

"You make it sound easy," Luciano objected in a dark tone. "I wouldn't like to go back empty-handed."

Tommaso sighed. Did he really feel the same way? In spite of the many arguments he used to encourage his friends, he would have felt badly defeated going back to Rome without the coveted bottle. He had to admit that to himself. He had put many hopes on that wine, even more so since Sara had entered the picture. By then, however, most of the game had already been played. It was almost over, and no external factor could affect the outcome.

Although he had meticulously done the math, he asked Roberta how much money they had. Her friend chuckled nervously, then sighed deeply.

"We have a very narrow margin. On the plus side, that bottle of Romanée-Conti is not the most valuable piece. Since not that many people are here, it might not even appeal to most of them."

"We can't know that for sure," Luciano emphasized.

"Of course, we can't."

"Come on, what's with the frowny faces?" Julie interjected. "This is not a funeral. We'll find out soon whether others are interested in that bottle. More importantly, which one of us will do the bidding?"

"You can do it if you'd like," Tommaso suggested.

"I'd like to, but I'm a little afraid I'll get confused," she replied, taking a step back.

"Okay. Any volunteer?"

"I'll do it," Roberta offered.

Tommaso sensed that behind her candidacy was a sense of guilt for not managing their money in the best way.

"You don't have to make up for anything, mind you." he pointed out. "We made every decision together, so let's enjoy the auction, and whatever happens, happens."

"Thank you, but I really want to do it."

"All right, then. Good luck, guys!"

"Good luck!" they all repeated.

Almost as if that was the signal, auctioneers and attendants made their entrance into the hall. People lowered their voices, and the auctioneer—a slender young man with horn-rimmed glasses, wearing a red suit and gray tie—thanked the audience and started the auction.

One after another, very quickly, single bottles or even entire cases of fine wines went up for auction. The words and gestures of the auctioneer had a hypnotic quality to them. The four friends were familiar with some labels but had only heard about others. The auction began to come alive, and some lots were sold for prices way above expectations (according to a small group of connoisseurs a couple of rows behind them).

As the main event approached, the tension became more and more palpable. Tommaso would have loved to enjoy what was happening around him with the same fascination of a mere spectator, but with each lot the auctioneer introduced—like the chiming of a clock—he became more nervous. The way he felt was only comparable to what he experienced when he met with Sara.

A small crowd of curious spectators had formed down the hall, near the entrance corridor, to follow the action. At one point, on the penultimate lot before the Romanée-Conti, two bidders engaged in a real fight to the death. They were contending a bottle of 1951 Penfolds Grange Hermitage amidst waving catalogs and admiring exclamations. Apparently, a young couple and a foreign customer represented by one of the operators on the phone both wanted that wine. Tommaso immediately understood that the couple had come to win that very bottle, and they did not intend to give it up. The tension became palpable and ran through the entire room like electricity. The auctioneer himself, though calm and professional, seemed involved in the battle. The two parties continued to raise their bids until the coveted prize was finally sold to the anonymous buyer on the phone for thirty-two thousand pounds.

A long applause rose in the hall, but it was not enough to completely cover the couple's expression of disappointment. Tommaso sensed a strong dose of frustration and displeasure in their stifled murmur. Many spectators began to get up since they had come solely for that highlight. The couple was also preparing to leave the hall. The man got up as if he had suddenly lost all interest in the event and got bored. His partner, holding her Burberry trench coat under her arm, held him back to slip the garment on. The auctioneer announced the new lot: the 1991 Romanée-Conti. The hall fell silent again, and the couple returned to their seats.

CHAPTER 29

"I am the one who keeps the taste of grapes on his lips. Bruised
bunches. Vermilion bites."
Pablo Neruda

Although Tommaso tried not to be overwhelmed by the
solemn moment, he felt his heart race. Instinctively, he
placed a hand on Julie's and received an encouraging smile.
He leaned forward and to the side to look at Roberta and
Luciano. They were both still, their eyes glued on the
auctioneer. He reached out a hand to squeeze his friend's
arm.

"It's our turn," she said in a hushed voice.

"The Penfolds thinned out the audience. The ones left
look more curious than competitors to me. We could
probably get away," said Luciano, attempting to add some
courage.

"Quiet, it's starting!" shushed Roberta.

After the epic battle for the Penfolds, the auctioneer
regained his composure. The tension in the hall had indeed
subsided, and Luciano was right.

Just watch and see! We are really going to make it, thought
Tommaso.

The auctioneer introduced the Romanée-Conti.

There it was, at last. Our Grail!

The starting price was announced, and after a brief
moment of hesitation, Roberta raised her hand. The
auctioneer pointed to her, eyeing the new offer. Roberta
looked at her friends and was astonished at how simple the
process was.

Tommaso felt like time was frozen and realized he had
been holding his breath the entire time. His body was still,

but his mind galloped forward, savoring the moment they could get their hands on the bottle.

No one was bidding, and no one seemed interested. It looked like the Romanée-Conti was there just for them, and the auction had been nothing more than a formality.

Suddenly, there was a turn of events.

The auctioneer asked if there were any other bids. Roberta smiled. The couple sitting behind them said something in a low voice. It seemed to Tommaso that the man wanted to deter his partner, but she insisted. The auctioneer pointed to the couple, acknowledging the new offer.

Roberta shuddered. She looked back at the couple, then back at the auctioneer. They still had a margin to raise the offer. The Romanée-Conti was evidently just a whim for the couple. They would not go any further. Roberta raised her hand again. The auctioneer took note of the raise and announced it.

The friends waited painfully for the moment to pass, but time seemed to stretch on forever. Once again, the couple behind them squabbled under their breath and raised their offer again. The auctioneer smiled and informed the room of the new amount.

Roberta looked at her friends. She was pale and kept nervously twisting her earring. When she spoke, her mouth was dry.

"I can make one last offer, but then on the way back, we'll really have to tighten our belts," she said in a hushed voice. "What should I do?"

"Raise the offer!" urged Julie, who was turning pale.

"Yes, go ahead!" confirmed Luciano.

"Let's go!" said Tommaso.

Roberta raised her hand. Her gesture drew a murmur of approval from some of the people in the room.

Tommaso strained his ear, trying to eavesdrop on the couple's reaction behind them. He was relieved when he heard the girl utter an exclamation of clear surrender.

The auctioneer looked at them and smiled.

It's done! Mission accomplished!

Unfortunately, that unexpected contention had sparked the attention of other spectators who, until a moment before, appeared to be completely uninterested. Tommaso thought they looked like a pack of hungry hyenas who woke up attracted by the smell of blood.

In an instant, the bidding started again, and the bottle, which they had pictured already in their hands, was bought, after a brief dispute, by an elderly gentleman. He was on his phone, wearing a blue blazer, a scarf around his neck, and Vicuna pants, probably on the line with the real buyer, who was most likely miles away.

They had been outbid.

The auctioneer introduced the next lot as they sat in silence. None of them had the courage to look at their friends' faces. Roberta was nothing more than a wax statue; Luciano had his gaze fixed forward; Julie had her arms crossed over her chest in a gesture of childish defense against the harshness of reality. Tommaso waited for his heartbeat to regain its regular rhythm after being sent into a tailspin by that emotional roller coaster.

He remembered a phrase he had read years earlier, "The bitterness of defeat is always much greater than the joy of victory." It was true. That was indeed the case. There was no use in rationalizing and repeating themselves that, after all, it was just a bottle of wine. Their hearts felt differently.

Now what?

They had to get up, leave that room—which had become empty and sad in a flash—and return to the hotel while exchanging fake smiles and mutual encouragement. Once home, someone would pat them on the back, telling them it would go better next time, even though everyone would know it wasn't true. There was not going to be a next time.

Julie was the first to break the silence. She placed a hand on Roberta's shoulder and rocked her gently. When her friend turned to look at her, her face was pale and tense.

"I'm sorry, I'm so sorry."

They all huddled around her. They tried to comfort her but could not come up with anything substantial. Then they realized it was best to give her time to process what happened and walked away so as not to further fuel the tension. Their adventure had come to an end. Luciano had a bitter grimace, while Tommaso felt chagrined. He was surprised by his and his friends' reactions, but, at the same time, he could not say or do anything to iron out that very unpleasant situation.

"I should have kept our finances in check," Roberta suddenly said. "I promised, but I didn't."

"We all agreed to enjoy the evening," Tommaso objected. A moment later, not having a definite plan, he went in the opposite direction. "I mean, sure. If we had saved money on dinner the second night, perhaps..."

"Look, let's all knock it off!" blurted Julie. "It was nobody's fault. We made every decision together. Traveling is expensive. We knew that. We would have spent a lot even if we had flown to London. The plan was to save money on hotels and enjoy meals and drinks, which we did. Personally, I don't regret anything. Things didn't work out. We have to deal with it. It happens."

Luciano nodded, albeit unconvinced.

"I know you're right, but I cared about that bottle."

"We all cared about it," replied Julie. "That's what we came here for. Now, let's put a cap on it."

"Let's put a tombstone on it," said Luciano in a low voice.

"What do we do now?" asked Tommaso. "On the bright side, we saved some money. We can take the tube and go to..."

He didn't finish the sentence. Where could they go? London didn't feel the same anymore. Every corner, even the most beautiful, would remind them of their defeat. No one said a word, but it was clear what was going through their minds.

"If it's okay with you guys," Roberta said finally, "I would gladly go back."

"To the hotel?" asked Julie.

Roberta cleared her throat.

"Home."

She was so sad that no one felt like talking her out of it. Truth be told, at that point, they all wanted to go home.

CHAPTER 30

"Memories are like wine decanting inside the bottle. They stay clear and the cloudiness remains at the bottom. One must not shake the bottle."
Mario Rigoni Stern

They returned to their hotel in a taxi. They didn't even change their clothes as they hurriedly packed their luggage, paid the bill, and hit the road.

Leaving London was a nightmare. The traffic was appalling, and they were still fractious from recent events. Luciano, who had preferred to get behind the wheel to work off his frustration, took a wrong turn and was forced to divert to the Victoria Station area, where they got stuck for a while. By the time they got out of traffic, the sun was setting. Luciano drove nonstop until they reached Folkstone, determined to catch up on lost time. They arrived at dinnertime and embarked immediately without delay. They took turns going to the toilet only after they boarded the shuttle.

When they reached Calais, they bought sandwiches, crackers, and a few beers, which they ate in the vehicle without stopping. On their way to Reims, as Tommaso was driving, it started raining heavily and soon turned into a violent storm. They were forced to pull over near a clearing in total darkness and wait for the weather to improve. The temperature had dropped, and they had to squirm inside the vehicle to get their coats.

"It's really pouring down, huh? I've seen many horror movies start with much less," commented Roberta.

"Please stop. I'm scared enough already," protested Julie.

"I'm here to protect you, maidens," yawned Luciano.

"Actually, you'd probably scare off possible attackers with your snoring!"

"Me? Snoring?"

"They're sitting in the front, and they don't hear it because of the engine noise, but I do," replied Roberta. "Come on, make yourself useful. Let me lean my head against your shoulder. I'm cold."

Soon after that conversation, Tommaso could hear the sound of two people breathing heavily. He looked in the rearview mirror and saw Luciano and Roberta sleeping on each other's shoulders. He felt a sense of relief.

"How are you?" Julie asked him.

The rain that battered on the car nacelle made the sound of their words intimate.

"I'm good. Still a little bewildered, actually. I'm also worried about this weather. If it keeps storming like this, it's going to be tough driving back. I should have checked the weather before we left, but with all that hurry, I didn't really think about it."

"None of us thought about it, for that matter. We all just wanted to go home. We look like sad little puppies, and that's a shame because I enjoyed the trip. In fact, you know what? I would do it again—maybe without the stress of an auction next time."

They both smiled.

"Do you think we're safe here?" she asked him, suddenly getting serious.

"Do you think anyone is around on a night like this?"

Julie yawned.

"Sorry. I'm getting sleepy."

"Why don't you get some sleep? Today was a hard day for you, too."

"I want to keep you company."

"I'm not sleepy. I'll keep watch. In that way, if a werewolf shows up, I can duck out first."

She playfully punched him on the shoulder then her phone rang as she received a text message. Julie pulled her smartphone out of her backpack and looked at it. Her face lit up.

"Is that Arnaud?" Tommaso asked, not able to hold back.

Without taking her eyes off the display, Julie nodded. She quickly answered the text, clucking her tongue between her teeth, then turned off the phone and huddled on the seat, using her coat as a blanket. She reached out her hand and placed it on Tommaso's.

"Does it bother you?"

"No, not at all."

The girl closed her eyes, and for a while, Tommaso looked at her. She looked happy. He envied her. He finished a sandwich, drank some of the now-warm beer, and tried to make himself comfortable.

The monotony of the roars had a soothing effect.

I'll try to get some rest too.

He fell asleep clutching his friend's hand. She was a real friend he did not know he had before going on that trip. When he woke up, it had stopped raining. It was late at night, and the countryside was dark. His friends were still asleep. He checked the GPS, then gulped down half a bottle of mineral water and started the engine, driving off gently to let the others continue to sleep. At that hour, no one was on the road. After taking a nap on the car seat, he felt rested and fit. He decided to aim for Chambéry. Driving in the silence of the night helped him relax his nerves and ponder.

Had it been that bad? He understood his friends' bitterness—or at least Roberta and Luciano's—but he was not sure he shared it. Not entirely, at least. In retrospect, going to the auction had been fun, and apart from the less-than-satisfactory outcome, it was also educational. Honestly, it had been exciting. He had felt the tension, the struggle, the desire to own that bottle in the air. Unfortunately, as an old saying goes, when two dogs fight over a bone, a third one runs away with it, and that is what happened. Perhaps, the lucky owner was enjoying the Romanée-Conti bottle at that very moment.

At that thought, Tommaso burst out laughing, and Julie opened her eyes.

"Where are we?" she asked, still sleepy.

"Near Troyes. How are you?"

"Fine," she replied, stretching. She turned to the backseat. "Those two are still asleep."

"Let them sleep. You are all in good hands. Your driver has a firm grip on the steering wheel, and he's taking you home."

"My Ulysses! Do you want me to take over?"

"No, I'm going like a train. You can keep texting Arnaud."

"You're an idiot!"

They both laughed, then Julie became serious. Tommaso looked at her from the corner of his eye and noticed.

"You have found a true friend," he merely told her.

Julie tightened her lips.

"Maybe I have embarked on a journey within the journey. We'll see."

The lights of Troyes appeared on the horizon. When Tommaso stopped the car at a gas station, Roberta woke up, followed by Luciano a few moments later. They were still dazed, but a stop at the roadside diner for a snack and some coffee put them back on track. Luciano offered to drive, and Roberta acted as his navigator. Tommaso and Julie settled in the backseat.

When Tommaso opened his eyes again, the sky was bright, and the car was parked at a lay-by, surrounded by nothing but the countryside. The car doors were open, and fresh air blew in. His three friends were sitting on a small wall by the side of the road near a stream of water that gurgled peacefully. When they saw he was awake, they waved to him. Apparently, they had been waiting for him. In the meantime, they had set up the little wall with some tissues, on which they had arranged the sandwiches they had purchased a few hours earlier.

Tommaso got out of the car and wrapped in his overcoat. The grass was fragrant and still wet with rain. The nature around him felt purified, renewed, and had a good smell to it. He sat down next to Luciano.

"Good morning! Ready for a proper snack?"

"I'm always ready for good things." He took a bite of a brioche and looked at his friends. "Feeling better?"

"Let's just say that sleeping helped me get over the beating," Roberta acknowledged. "I still want to apologize to you, though..."

A chorus of playful protests silenced her.

"Knock it off, or we'll leave you here," Luciano threatened her affectionately. Then he stood up and addressed his friends.

"However, I'm the one who needs to apologize to all of you for how I reacted yesterday afternoon. I was very disappointed, and I think it showed. However, I slept on it, and when I woke up, I realized I was overjoyed to be here with you. Moreover, if we had won the auction, we probably wouldn't be here right now in this beautiful place, enjoying an improvised picnic. Also, as Tommaso said yesterday, on the bright side, we saved money. With that money, I could actually organize my notorious trip to Japan. What I'm trying to say is—some people say it is impossible to know how much good can come from a bad situation, and I agree. Hold it, hold it, no applause, please. This isn't just a circumstantial speech."

"It sure sounds like it to me," Julie teased him, nibbling on a slice of cake.

"It doesn't. And to prove it to you..." Luciano returned to the car, opened the trunk, and pulled out the Clavelier bottle of Combe D'Orveaux.

"To prove it to you, I want to uncork and drink this bottle of wine with you. I meant to take this home, but I want to share it with you guys."

"What? You said you wanted to drink that with your girlfriend," said Roberta.

"Yes, but it's better to drink it now with all of you together."

"She would have liked it..."

"No doubt, but she probably wouldn't have *appreciated* it. Not like us, anyway."

There wasn't much more to add. They uncorked the bottle and poured the content into large paper cups they originally bought for beer when they stopped in Calais. Facing the deep green French countryside, they toasted to their adventure and to the sense of friendship they felt as renewed as that fresh morning.

Tommaso and Julie's half-hearted protests about the time Luciano had decided to drink had been for nothing. There is always a good reason to toast. At that moment, theirs was that their palates were rested from the night of sleep and could savor the sweet notes in the wine.

CHAPTER 31

"I like on the table, when we're speaking,
the light of a bottle of intelligent wine"
Pablo Neruda

The rest of the journey was significantly smoother. The weather had improved, and by the afternoon, the sun had reappeared in the sky. The roads were clear, and the drive back to Italy was effortless. They stopped at a diner in Turin for refreshments, where Tommaso received a message from Sara. He waited a few seconds before reading it.

Then, while holding his mobile phone under the edge of the table, he quickly scanned the text on the screen. Although he did not have any high expectations, he still felt dejected. Sara only messaged him to ask if they succeeded in buying the Romanée-Conti bottle. He stared at his phone for a while, undecided about what and how to reply. Lying did not suit him, but neither did admitting defeat, so he opted to stall.

As he observed Julie, he mused with a hint of jealousy (which made him uncomfortable) how well she was dealing with the situation. Her drive home was less bitter because of the texts she kept exchanging with Arnaud.

Once they got back into the car and he settled in the back seat, he replied to Sara. He told her the truth. It had been a good trip, full of interesting events, but unfortunately, they were not successful. The bids for the bottle had gone up beyond their reach. After he sent the message, he was relieved that he told the truth. If what had happened would belittle him in the eyes of Sara, so be it!

He was disappointed, but he could not really do anything about it.

"Tommy, we have some unfinished business," Julie suddenly said as she waved her hand out the window.

"That sounds juicy," Roberta said, jumping at the chance to tease her friend.

"Speaking of juicy, I think you win across the board, Roby," Luciano intervened, winking at his friend, who blushed.

"What are you referring to?" Tommaso finally managed to say.

"I'm talking about your cinematic dreams. You've been saying you've been having strange, absurd dreams for days. Dreams that 'if only Spielberg knew'... It's time to tell us about them. Go on. Entertain us!"

"He told me about these dreams a few times, but he's never described them to me," Luciano backed her up.

"Okay, let it out. Spill the beans!"

Roberta leaned into the back seat and tried to tickle Tommaso, who had to crouch in the corner of the car.

"Okay, but I'm warning you, after you hear them, you'll wish you had never asked me."

"Or maybe we'll just realize our friend is a dangerous sociopath," laughed Julie. That time, it was her turn to get tickled, then Tommaso put his arm around her shoulders. The two of them stayed in that position as he narrated his dreams.

"Before we left, I dreamt we were robbing a bank to get money for the bottle, but it was totally absurd," he exclaimed, rather embarrassed. He recounted his dream in full detail amidst questions and jokes from his friends.

"What did we have on our faces? Playing cards? Dude, you are a weirdo," Luciano burst out laughing until he had tears in his eyes.

"'Hey! Eyes on the road!" scolded Roberta.

"Yeah, and then I was shooting this guy. He was some kind of bank concierge, but he wouldn't die, so we made a deal. He would play dead, and I would let him go." Tommaso kept going on and on. "Then we had a meeting with the director, and he invited us to spend the night there."

They made it to Rome in the evening. The weather was unusually mild, and the city seemed to have a different scent.

They dropped Roberta off first, pulled up in front of her place, and got out of the car to say goodbye. They hugged affectionately.

"In my opinion, we did well," said Luciano, summing up how everyone felt.

"We did everything we set out to do, and frankly, as far as I'm concerned, many things even exceeded my expectations. Yesterday I felt like we missed our grand finale, but today, I am not so convinced about that anymore. At the cost of pointing out the obvious, I've realized so many things in the last few hours that I wouldn't have had a chance to understand if everything had gone smoothly."

They hugged again.

Fifteen minutes later, Tommaso gave Julie his special goodbye.

"Thank you for your support. And as for everything else…"

Before Tommaso could finish the sentence, she smiled and shushed him by putting a finger on his lips. Then she got on her toes and kissed him on the cheek.

"I'll see you soon," she told him.

As he watched her walk away, Tommaso felt a deep sense of gratitude for what that trip had meant to him.

CHAPTER 32

"Years, lovers, and glasses of wine. These are things that should never be counted."
Ellis Jones

After a night of dreamless sleep, Monday morning seemed to come crashing down on him. At home, lying on his bed with his eyes fixed on the ceiling, Tommaso tried to convince himself that he really needed to go to his office to resume his daily routine. However, the mere idea of seeing Piergiorgio again and being teased by him was very discouraging.

He went out with his head still immersed in memories of the trip, so much so that he had to turn around twice and go back inside his apartment, the first time to get his overcoat, then his cell phone. Nevertheless, he was so afraid of being late that he arrived at the office early. He stopped in front of the entrance to the building, undecided whether to go in. Around him, the cold, damp wind was lifting piles of yellow and rust-colored leaves, moving them from the sidewalk to the street and back again. He turned his gaze toward the busy street, and for a moment, he thought he spotted Sara at the entrance to the bar across the street.

This thing really got to me. I'm even hallucinating now.

Sara's ghost waved in his direction. It was really her and she was greeting him. Suddenly, the cold wind, traffic noise, smog, and dead leaves disappeared, making way for a sudden spring. Caught by surprise, he waved back at her and crossed the street to join her, ignoring the red sedan that passed within an inch of him and almost ran him over.

"Hey!" exclaimed the girl when he reached her. "I guess you're not loving the idea of going back to work but killing yourself seems a bit excessive."

"What are you doing here?" He asked her. It was the only sentence that came out of his mouth as if he had forgotten that Sara often went to their office carrying files and folders containing documents.

I shouldn't get worked up. She's most probably here for a meeting with Piergiorgio, he thought before even giving her time to respond.

"I was waiting for you. I wanted to welcome you back," she said, blushing a little. Her reply surprised Tommaso, who smiled carefully and asked her to have breakfast with him.

"Sure, I'd like that. I wanna hear all about your great adventure through Europe."

They entered the café and found a seat in a corner, far enough away from the crowded counter. After ordering cappuccinos and croissants, Sara stared him straight in the eye and said,

"So, the auction did not go well..."

Tommaso failed to catch any particular nuance in her gaze. He was still in shock that he was sitting in the company of his goddess.

"No, unfortunately not. As it turned out, our budget was not enough to compete with the bids someone started making at some point. It was fun, though."

He told her in full detail how the auction had unfolded. They laughed together as Tommaso—now free of all tension and bitterness—recounted the stages of his fiasco. Encouraged by how interested she seemed, he began to tell her about all the stops they took over the course of the journey, the wines and foods they tasted, and the colors of the vineyards. Suddenly, as if struck by an epiphany, he stopped and asked her, "Listen, why don't you join me and my friends for a drink sometime? That way, we can tell you about all the beautiful things we've seen." He looked at her hesitantly. "If you feel like it, that is."

"Of course. I'd like that!" she answered enthusiastically. "I had to hold back from texting you too much over the last few days because I didn't want to disturb you, but clearly, I want to know everything about your trip. Every little detail."

Tommaso felt revived.

"You should have texted me. I would have been very happy about it. After all, although I was with a group of friends, I was there—alone."

He barely whispered those last few words, but they seemed to break through the girl's heart as she blushed and smiled again.

"We also took a lot of pictures. And we bought some bottles that we could drink together. Of course, I would have preferred to drink the Romanée-Conti with you, but..."

"I wouldn't rule it out. It might still happen."

Tommaso looked at her, baffled. He was not sure what was going on. Was it possible that regardless of everything he told her, Sara did not understand what happened in London?

"I must let you in on a little secret. We have the Romanée-Conti."

"What? Who's we?" asked Tommaso, increasingly confused.

Sara's eyes glittered.

"We. You and me."

Tommaso shook his head. His heart was pounding. That 'we' spoken by Sara made the whole room spin for him.

"Forgive me, Sara, but I'm not getting it..."

She reached across the table and touched his index finger with hers.

"Remember the bottle of Romanée-Conti up for auction on that website? I purchased it. Or, rather, my boss bought it for me—because I wanted it for you."

Tommaso remained motionless for a few seconds, then felt his lips stretch and widen to infinity.

"Explain everything, please."

"You told me about the online auction. I got curious and checked it out. The bottle was still there, and no one had bought it yet. The next day, my boss closed a very profitable and important deal, mostly because of my work. He asked me what I would like to receive as a bonus. I put two and two together and..."

"Two and two?"

Tommaso couldn't believe his ears.

"Well, I asked him to buy that wine. I was afraid you might lose it. Maybe it sounds silly to you now, but at the time—I mean, you cared so much about it, and I didn't want someone to take it from you. The way you spoke about the bottle finally convinced me to do something a little crazy myself."

She looked at him, a little fearful.

"Did I do wrong?"

Tommaso could no longer feel the ground beneath his feet.

"You purchased the Romanée-Conti...for me?"

"I did."

Sara lifted her backpack and pulled out the bottle, gently placing it between the coffee cups and breakfast leftovers.

"This isn't a joke, is it?" muttered Tommaso, still in disbelief. "I hope it's not a counterfeit bottle."

Sara laughed and showed him every detail of the bottle.

He had traveled around Europe to find something he already owned, and it was just a stone's throw from his heart. Without letting go of Sara's hand, he gently ran his fingers over the label with his other hand.

"Sara, I swear. I would go to London and lose that auction ten thousand more times just to spend another moment like this with you. You are completely crazy! A lovely, unique, wonderful crazy person!"

He leaned forward and kissed her without considering the possible consequences or minding the stares of the other customers in the café. She did not flinch. A ray of sunlight came through the window, resting on the bottle of 1991 Romanée-Conti and making it shine.

CHAPTER 33

"That's the problem with drinking, I thought, as I poured myself a drink.
If something bad happens you drink in an attempt to forget;
if something good happens you drink in order to celebrate;
and if nothing happens you drink to make something happen."
Charles Bukowski

That very evening, Tommaso joined his friends at the place where Julie worked. Sara came along. He called them one by one, summoning them to a special meeting. He had an important announcement to make. Upon seeing him arrive with the girl, his friends immediately started speculating, thinking they had figured out what type of announcement he wanted to make.

After introductions, with appetizers on the table, Tommaso asked Roberta to tell Sara about what happened at the auction.

The disappointment she had felt was now behind her. She threw in a mix of jokes and grimaces to reconstruct every phase of what they had experienced. She depicted the event as something from the movie *Mission: Impossible,* and in reality, it did turn out to be an impossible mission. When she got to the point where the last offer had utterly mocked them, Tommaso interrupted her.

"Wait, wait!" Luciano protested. "Now comes the highlight of the evening. When we thought the bottle was already ours, and they stole it from under our noses!"

Tommaso smiled.

"I would let her continue if that were how things really went, but we didn't lose the bottle."

His friends looked at him, puzzled. At that point, Sara, who had prior instructions from Tommaso, took the bottle from her backpack and put it solemnly at the center of the table.

Luciano leaped to his feet and burst out laughing. Roberta shook her head, struggling to realize what just happened.

Julie grabbed the bottle to verify its authenticity. They seemed to be standing before an apparition. Then again, it kind of was. Tommaso thought they would remember that moment for the rest of their lives. They hit Sara with a whirlwind of questions. At first, she was shy, but then Tommaso encouraged her, and she proudly unraveled the mystery of the bottle they had wanted so badly.

Eventually, they all stood in silence, gazing at the Romanée-Conti.

"You've had it all along," said Luciano after a few seconds.

"The Grail, in the end, has always been yours, thanks to this divine young lady."

"I wanted to tell you right away," Sara apologized, "but I wasn't sure my initiative would have pleased Tommaso. I knew he was planning this trip with you guys. So, in the end, I preferred to stay quiet about it. However, when I heard the auction didn't go well..."

There was a round of applause.

"Thank you for sharing the Grail with us as well," Roberta added, and the others backed her up.

"I considered every possible reason for this meeting, but I would have never imagined I would be drinking some Romanée-Conti wine from 1991!" remarked Julie as she gave them the glasses.

Tommaso had the honor of uncorking the bottle and did so with the respect and reverence reserved for a dream come true. The tasting exceeded the group's already high expectations. They were all enraptured and agreed that the moment was one of the most unforgettable of their lives. In an odd twist of fate, Tommaso appeared to be the least excited. After all, this whole story had started with him. Yet, how could one blame him? With all due respect to the hallowed Romanée-Conti, he had already found his own personal Grail that very morning, and now she was sitting next to him, smiling at him.

ACKNOWLEDGEMENTS

A dutiful and grateful mention to Roberta V. and Stefania G. for having inspired the characters of Roberta, to Vinicio Z. for Luciano, to Anna M. for Julie and as for Tommaso... well, of course, that's me!

This book most certainly owes a lot to a few people.
First and foremost, Roberta Viotti, a friend, and companion of a thousand wine tastings, who accommodated all my requests regarding the re-reading of the novel.

Many thanks to my friends Andrea Rondena, Massimiliano Giordano, Ilaria Ranucci, Tommaso Loriga, Sara Nizzola, Elena Medori, and the "White Flowers" group for giving me advice on the drafting of the text.

Finally, a big thank you to Antonio Erba and Giorgio Fogliani for technical advice and Luca Casadei for editing and narrative advice.

Printed in Great Britain
by Amazon